THE VISITATIO

Ahmed Essop
THE VISITATION

Ravan Press   Johannesburg

Published by Ravan Press (Pty) Ltd.
409 — 416 Dunwell, 35 Jorissen Street
Braamfontein, Johannesburg 2001, South Africa
© Copyright Ahmed Essop
First Impression August 1980
Cover drawing by Richard Jack
Typesetting: Sandy Parker
ISBN 0 86975 182 4 (cloth)
ISBN 0 86975 183 2 (paper)
Printed by Heer Printing Co. (Pty) Ltd., Pretoria

For Lionel Abrahams

One

Mr Emir Sufi was an undersized man who had grown obese over the years because of his penchant for sweetmeats. He was a wealthy man, owning several apartment buildings in Fordsburg. His daily life revolved around three pastimes: women, driving one of his motor-cars — the Jaguar was his favourite — and visiting cinemas. Besides his wife who lived in 'Orient Mansions' in Terrace Road, he kept a concubine in each of his apartment buildings. His motor-cars (he replaced the old ones whenever new models made their appearance in dealers' show-rooms) were usually parked in the spacious basement of 'Orient Mansions'. All his cars were nut-brown in colour; all his suits were shades of brown. He was essentially an unassuming man. One never saw him in public places in the company of his women as he firmly believed that home was the proper place for them and their company only to be enjoyed in the privacy of bedrooms; but his belief was knotted with the fear that exposure of them would unleash in undisciplined men curiosity, envy and hate. Blessed with all he needed, he led a quiet dignified life.

To Gool, the gangster, Mr Sufi presented himself as mellow prey. He needed what Gool termed 'protection', and so he found himself included in the select group of merchants and landlords who enjoyed Gool's patronage.

With Mr Sufi the payment of the monthly 'protection fee' to Gool was a social ritual: by having it so, he preserved his dignity. He would be at 'Orient Mansions' on the last day of every month. Fawzia, his daughter, would prepare all the delicacies

1

required for the occasion. About eight in the evening a bell would ring and Mr Sufi, standing nervously on the balcony, would go towards the wrought-iron gate that gave access to the landing and the stairs. He would open the gate, welcome his visitor by shaking his hand, and lead him along the balcony towards a double-door — its upper half gleaming with stained-glass lozenges — that gave entry into a large sitting-room which was lavishly furnished and mainly used for guests. Mr Sufi and his family occupied the entire top floor of 'Orient Mansions', consisting of the guests' room, six bedrooms, a living-room, a large dining-room, a well-equipped kitchen, several bathrooms, a reception room for tenants and an office.

On these occasions, while pouring tea and offering delicacies to Gool, he would talk about films and film-stars, motor-cars, the weather, cricket and soccer, but never asked Gool any personal questions. After half an hour Fawzia would enter the room with a silver tray on which lay an envelope. Mr Sufi would take the envelope, stand up, shake hands with his visitor, give him the envelope as though he were conferring an award, and lead him out. He would unlock the gate and shake Gool's hand once more before he departed.

Gool would make his way down the unlit stairs, holding on to the railing to give him anchorage should he miss a step. If there was one thing Mr Sufi was doggedly courageous about it was his refusal to have the stairs illuminated, not even for the gangster's sake. All the stairs, foyers and corridors of his apartment buildings — most of them three-storeyed structures, rather old and in need of renovation — were unlit. He was obsessed by the idea that a continuously burning lamp was not only a waste of electricity — in his personal creed waste was allied to nihilism — but a fatal drain on his bank account in the form of municipal charges. Should any of his tenants complain of the difficulty of using stairs in the dark he would be overcome by a squall of inner turbulence and curtly dismiss the complaint with the pessimistic declaration that the grave was a murky place.

Mr Sufi's relationship with Gool was restricted to the monthly visit. Should he see him in the streets, at the mosque or in the foyers of cinemas, he would try to avoid him, but if the meeting was unavoidable, he would lift his hand in recognition, say a word or two and depart. He carefully avoided shaking Gool's hand in public as he did not wish to give people the impression that he was on friendly terms with the man.

Gool was of average height, tawny in complexion, with leaf-flat glossy black hair and a fastidiously trimmed moustache. He was always sprucely dressed in a suit, even when summer temperatures were unrelenting. He was reputed to be a wealthy man. His main sources of revenue were the gambling clubs in Fordsburg, Pageview, Newtown and Mayfair. Once a month he received a harvest of 'protection fees' from the various club-owners. He also collected 'fees' from affluent individuals during social visits like his monthly call on Mr Sufi. At times he engaged in commercial dealings, but his true acumen was displayed in activities of the type described as 'back door trading'. On occasion he played the role of a peace-maker among feuding families and was liberally 'rewarded' by the parties involved for restoring peace.

Over the years Gool had subtly integrated his activities into the life of the community and developed his methods into an art. There was nothing of youthful vainglory about him; neither did he display the uncontrolled instincts of a desperado nor the overt cupidity of a run-of-the-mill gang-leader. Refined in manners, judicious and crafty — usually restrained, he was capable of uncoiling in an occasional display of swift, calculated brutality that took his opponents by surprise — he was feared and respected. At times he took up the cause of the weak and the poor — he redressed wrongs and dispensed charity. He had been to jail for a brief spell, but that was for taking part in a passive resistance campaign organised by the Orient Front. His gang was not known by any spectacular name, and therefore did not project an image of lawlessness and savagery. His own name stood for his gang's. If someone said, 'I shall call Gool,' or 'Gool is with me,' he meant a gang. Gool so completely overshadowed his gang members that to many people he seemed imbued with superhuman power.

One evening Mr Sufi's relationship with Gool underwent a profound change. Gool made his usual visit but did not depart after receiving the envelope.

'Your sweetmeats are delicious, Mr Sufi. Does your daughter make them?'

Gool sat down on a chair and took a red sweetmeat encrusted with pistachio nuts. Mr Sufi, nervous at the inquiry, sat down as well.

'She is a lovely girl,' Gool said, biting into the delicacy.

3

Mr Sufi looked at his guest with trepidation.

'How are your other women getting on?'

'They are well,' Mr Sufi replied feebly, stretching his hand on a sudden impulse to take a chocolate-coated éclair. He crushed the éclair and the cream frothed over his fingers. He stuffed it into his mouth.

'Here is a serviette,' Gool said with a smile, and offered him one.

Mr Sufi wiped his fingers and mouth.

'I'm expecting a phone call here. Any minute now,' Gool said, looking at his watch.

Mr Sufi's body stiffened as though something fatal were about to happen. His mind reeled with the menacing possibilities of the prearranged telephone call. Was there a plot to kidnap him? Or Fawzia? Or was Gool's gang going to ravish his concubines while he was held captive in his own home? Or was Gool trying to implicate him in a murder?

The telephone rang and Mr Sufi jumped up from his seat.

'Frightened you a bit,' Gool said, standing up and going towards the telephone.

'Yes . . . Hullo Akbar . . . Have they arrived? . . . Send them to "Orient Mansions" . . . Top floor . . . I am waiting.'

While Gool was talking over the telephone, Mr Sufi drank some tea to calm himself. Gool came back and said:

'You know, I thought of you this morning when I was told they were bringing a consignment of lamps. "Who else," I said to Akbar, "but my friend Mr Sufi would have use for them? I always have difficulty in using his stairs in the dark." '

'Lamps?'

'Yes, sometimes I get unusual things and then I think of my friends. You have so many flats to light up.'

He smiled and pointed to the cigar-case. Mr Sufi hurriedly gave him one.

'You'd best tell your daughter to open the gate. They will be here any moment. Have you an empty room?'

'Unfortunately not in this building.'

'This room is large enough. Tomorrow you can have them stored somewhere else. We could easily move some of the furniture. Come, let's get busy before they come.'

Gool stood up, but paused for a moment.

'The lamps could be left on the balcony if you wish.'

' 'No . . . This room will do,' Mr Sufi said, fearing the exposure of 'back door' goods.

With a show of eagerness, puffing and looking florid, Mr Sufi helped Gool shift the settee, armchairs and display cabinet.

Feeling faint, he told Gool that he was going to tell his daughter to open the gate, and left the room. He hurried to the bedroom, was relieved to find his wife not there and sat down on the dressing-table stool to assuage his agitation. He heard footsteps and, quickly grabbing a comb from the dressing-table, began to rake his balding cranium. A moment before his wife entered the room he realised his folly and put the comb down.

'Tell Fawzia to open the gate quickly. They are bringing some goods.'

His wife left, perplexed at finding her husband in the bedroom while Gool was still in the house.

Mr Sufi returned to the guests' room and was about to sit down when Fawzia came in and announced that the goods had arrived.

'Please tell them to bring the lamps here,' Gool said. 'We have made room.'

Fawzia left and after a few minutes five men in single file with boxes on their shoulders marched into the room. Gool directed the arranging of the boxes.

'How many?' Gool asked one of the men.

'Fifty.'

'Bring them all up,' he ordered. He opened one of the boxes, removed some of the plastic foam covering, carefully extracted a lamp and unwrapped it.

' "Apollo" . . . Lovely name . . . ' Gool mused, examining the picture of a statue of Apollo on the wrapper. 'Beautiful . . . Some sort of Greek god.'

'Yes,' Mr Sufi said, glancing at the picture without sharing Gool's aesthetic pleasure. He did not even attempt to recall, from his school days, who Apollo was.

More room had to be made. The furniture was packed closer, the carpets rolled up. The boxes were stacked to the ceiling. At last those who had brought the lamps left and Gool too took his leave.

On the stair landing Gool paused for a moment.

'A lamp is a wonderful thing, Mr Sufi. But it has a strange habit of blowing out at night when the shops are closed. Now your

5

flats and stairs will never be without lights. Your tenants will be grateful. Good night.'

And he descended into the gloom of the stairs.

Mr Sufi returned to his residence, looked at his bewildered wife and his four daughters, and said he was going to bed.

Mr Sufi's life-pattern had been so suddenly and severely torn that he felt he had been sucked into another world. But slowly, in the silent darkness of his bedroom, he came to himself and realised what had happened. Gool had converted his guests' room into a warehouse containing thousands of lamps. Thousands! He made a quick arithmetical calculation. If each box contained two hundred lamps and there were fifty boxes, then he now possessed ten thousand. He shivered at the thought of the vast number. What was he going to do with so many? He could not give them to his tenants for — besides the fact that such impulsive benevolence would give rise to suspicion and questions — his tenants replaced burnt-out lamps at their own expense. And as for lighting the stairs, foyers and corridors of his apartment buildings after so many years of eclipse . . . If the police arrested the thieves . . . He pulled the blankets over his head. God! If Gool had wanted more money he would gladly have given it to him. What had he done to deserve this affliction?

Perhaps he could take several boxes at a time in one of his cars and throw them over a precipice somewhere. The thought filled him with hope and he threw the blankets off him. He pressed the bedside lamp button and found, by a queer trick of fate, that the lamp failed to go on. He pressed the button several times in desperation. The lamp was burnt out. He thought of Gool's parting words (how prophetic!) and a spasm of fear gripped him. He felt his body oppressed by the darkness. He covered himself with the blankets. Gradually his fear thawed. It was perhaps a fortunate accident that his bedside lamp had failed, for what would people have thought of him if they had seen him carrying boxes into his car like a servant? And he would have had difficulty carrying the boxes down the unlit stairs. Perhaps he should leave the lamps where they were. If the police came he would tell them the truth.

When his wife came to bed he pretended to be asleep, and the pretence mercifully extended into the reality.

Next morning he told his wife to lock the guests' room and let no one in. In future the family's private living-room would be used for guests as well.

But throughout the next day Mr Sufi was troubled. The lamps had been illegally obtained and therefore he could neither use them nor dispose of them. He decided to appeal to Gool over the telephone. He would tell him that although he appreciated the lamps he had unfortunately nowhere to store them. He would be glad if he could arrange to have them taken away.

'You need lamps all the time,' Gool answered.

'The danger . . .'

'What danger while I'm around?'

'Please Gool, tell those who brought the lamps to take them away. I will pay them.'

'Mr Sufi, the lamps are a personal gift from me. Every night lamps blow out and in no time you will need some more.'

As Mr Sufi replaced the telephone a lamp seemed to blow out within *him*.

After a fortnight Mr Sufi, emerging from a cinema and going towards his car, was caught in a thunderstorm. He rushed into a nearby café. Gool, who was sitting at a table in the company of a lady, saw him and and called him to come over.

Mr Sufi was shocked to hear Gool's voice above the din of the storm. He looked towards a dimly-lit recess and saw Gool and the lady. Controlling his agitation as best he could, he went towards them.

'Come and have some coffee. Sit down,' Gool said.

'I am in a hurry . . . '

'Sit down and relax. Hurry kills.'

Gool poured coffee and passed the cup to Mr Sufi.

'Gloria,' Gool said to the lady, 'have you met my friend Mr Sufi?'

'I have heard of him,' she said, extending her hand to him across the table. She was a dusky woman, her face plastered with heavy make-up, her hair a thick sorrel-coloured mane.

'You are so handsome!' she exclaimed, admiring Mr Sufi's crescent-shaped sleek eyebrows and his liquid dark eyes fringed with long, almost feminine eyelashes.

Mr Sufi blushed and Gool said laughingly, 'Look at him, blushing like a schoolboy! No one would think he is an emir with a harem.'

'You are also very rich!' Gloria said emphatically, leaning over the table.

Mr Sufi looked embarrassed, but Gool rescued him, saying, 'She loves picnics. She is a wonderful cook. You must join us someday.'

'Yes, I will,' Mr Sufi said, hoping that he would never have to go with them.

'Mr Sufi,' Gloria said, 'you will make a wonderful cook's assistant. I shall insist that you help me.'

'You and Gloria will make a pretty pair,' Gool said. 'By the way, the lamps must be very useful to you.'

'Yes,' he answered, drinking coffee and trying to hold the cup still in his hands.

'What lamps?' Gloria inquired.

'Lamps to light up his apartment buildings.'

'How wonderful!' Gloria sang.

Mr Sufi forced a smile, but inwardly he was riled that Gool should have mentioned the lamps in the presence of Gloria. Soon everyone would know about them.

'Replace all the old lamps with new ones,' Gool said, 'and at night your buildings will look like those in New York.'

'Or San Francisco!' Gloria said, clicking two fingers. 'By the way, one of my friends stays in your building in Lilian Road. Do you know Hanif?'

'Yes,' Mr Sufi said, looking out of the window without bothering to recall the man. The storm had abated. 'You must excuse me now. I have to go.'

Gool extended his hand to him and so did Gloria who said, 'Don't forget to visit me sometime. Gool will tell you where to find me.' And she blew him a kiss.

Two

As the end of the month approached, Mr Sufi's fears began to swell. Gool would come on his usual visit and what explanation would he give him for having left the lamps in the guests' room? What would Gool say to him when he found the stairs and the foyer unlit? And what if Gool had received more lamps and decided to give them to him? Should he order the housemaids to store all the lamps in a spare bedroom and later, after Gool's departure, have them brought back? What if the police arrived while the lamps were being removed? His only defence would be lost. Mr Sufi was still undecided when the last day of the month arrived. Before the day ended he would have to do something. But he was saved when Gool telephoned and said, 'Mr Sufi, I am unable to come this evening as I have an important matter to attend to. Can you come to High Road now?'

'Not at your place Gool ... you understand ... I could meet you anywhere else.'

'Then meet me in fifteen minutes at the corner of Fox and Loveday Streets downtown. Bring your cheque book with you.'

Mr Sufi felt so relieved that Gool would not be visiting him — he would have another month to decide what to do with the lamps — that he decided to give Gool twice the usual fee.

When he reached the appointed place, Gool was waiting for him. There was another man with him. Mr Sufi had seen him many times before in Gool's company but had not met him. Gool shook hands and introduced him to Akbar. Akbar was tall and lean with a sharp-featured face; his sparse long hair was combed backwards

9

and lay curled over his coat collar.

'Mr Sufi has enough lamps to light up the city,' Gool said to Akbar above the din of the traffic. Akbar laughed.

'Come, I have a small business deal,' Gool said, placing his hand on Mr Sufi's shoulder. 'The place is not far from here. We can walk.'

They crossed two streets and entered an arcade. Mr Sufi could hear his heart thumping. They were somewhere in a labyrinth where garishly-coloured neon signs signalled frantically and hideous rock music pulsated from loudspeakers.

Gool stopped at a chemist's window and said:

'Look!'

A three-foot marble statuette of Apollo stood among bottles of ladies' perfumery and toilet preparations, garlanded with magenta ribbons.

'Beautiful. Do you recognise him?' Gool asked.

Mr Sufi looked without answering.

'I was correct. That's the Greek god. Don't you remember the picture on the lamp-wrapper?'

'Yes,' he answered, but, preoccupied with the business deal Gool had spoken of, made no attempt to recognise the similarity.

'That's Apollo. I wonder why they named the lamps after him? Perhaps he had something to do with light.'

Gool admired the statuette, then walked on.

They walked into a quiet street. Mr Sufi found himself in a motor-dealer's show-room standing before a red sports car with a retracted black hood.

'Here she is,' Gool said. 'A beauty.'

Mr Sufi looked at the sports car as though mesmerised. It was a vibrant scarlet, its body sleek, low-slung and missile-like in design. He walked around it and read the gilt letters below the manufacturer's emblem at the rear: Farina Spider. Exotic sports cars had always fascinated him, but he had stoically curbed the temptation to buy one as he felt that a sports car would not accord with his image of dignified affluence.

Gool opened the door on the driver's side, got in, opened the passenger's door and asked Mr Sufi to get in.

'Just the thing. Beautiful and fast. Feel the seats. Lovely and soft. Do you like it?'

Mr Sufi's hand glided over the upholstery.

'A little expensive,' Gool said, 'but what's a little expense

between friends? And it will do my image good,' he added with
a suppressed chuckle.

The salesman came up and Gool said to him:

'We'll take this beauty now. Get the papers ready.'

'What's the price?' Mr Sufi asked timidly, his heart lying in the
carpeted well where his shoes rested.

The salesman told him.

He took out his cheque book from his pocket, hastily signed
a page, handed it to the salesman, told Gool he had to take his
wife to a doctor, got out of the car and left the premises.

For the first few moments he felt happy at his escape, even
though his happiness had been gained at an exorbitant ransom.
But later, when he reached his car and drove into Fordsburg, he
felt bitter and angry with himself. He should have asserted his
manhood, defied the gangster's blackmail. He regretted he had not
opposed Gool many years ago when he had first come to him and
slyly proposed, during a friendly conversation, the 'protection'
he offered to certain selected individuals who, because of their
status and wealth, presented themselves as easy prey to the wicked
and the covetous. He should have taken up arms against that
proposal. Now he was placed in a defensive position. Still, he
had the power to parry with him. He could instruct the bank
not to honour the cheque. He could even go to the police and
inform them of the lamps. There was nothing to stop him. Only
in the cinema world did criminals triumph over good men. He
turned his car in the direction of the police-station. But a red
traffic robot not only prevented him going on, but signalled
disaster. Didn't he know that Gool was a master, that he
manipulated the police? Didn't he know what would happen
to him if he attempted to implicate Gool in a crime? Didn't he
know that several times Gool had been brought to court, but
invariably walked out a free man, free to revenge himself on
his enemies? He drove homewards, oppressed by the presentiment
that the sports car was a prelude to further blackmail.

On his way home he passed 'Nirvana Mansions', one of his
properties in Crown Road. His concubine Olga lived in the
building. Torn by rage and helplessness at being plundered by
Gool of a part of his wealth — so vital to the functioning of his
urban soul — he desperately craved for some diversion to forget
his loss. He turned his car and drove back to 'Nirvana Mansions'.
He parked at the entrance of the building and hurried up the

stairs.

Olga opened the apartment door. She was wearing a tangerine dress, a red scarf and a yellow apron. She had been in the kitchen where she was preparing lunch. Mr Sufi shut the door violently, and surprised her by gripping her waist and leading her to the bedroom. 'The food will burn,' she said, but he took no heed and entering the room, flung her on the bed.

Later, Olga freed herself, hurried to the kitchen and found it filled with acrid smoke.

Mr Sufi fell asleep. He woke in the evening and had a bath. Feeling physically refreshed — though the money spent on Gool's Spider still gnawed at him — and very hungry, he sat down to have supper with Olga. Feeling restless after supper, he decided to go with Olga for a drive to the Zoo Lake. She dressed, applied make-up and adorned herself with jewellery.

They reached the Zoo Lake and parked near some huge oak trees along the bank. The dark water lay tamely before them, its stillness occasionally broken by a waterfowl or the splash of water against a rock. The stillness of the lake reminded him of the lamps, the journey to the motor-dealer and his own state of inner devastation. He remained silent, longing to confide in Olga, to say, 'I have a problem. What shall I do?' But he had never made confidantes of his concubines. Besides, it would have been a reduction of his manhood to seek help from them.

He drove back to Fordsburg, though Olga would have liked to walk with him along the lake's banks.

In the apartment Olga undressed. She was a well-shaped woman, her skin the colour of tawny sand. Her glossy mass of bronze curls matched her eyes perfectly. Her entire appearance was one of mellowness and earthy richness.

'You are troubled, Emir,' she said softly, sitting down beside him and taking his hand in hers. It was with stoic self-restraint that he refrained from telling her of his burden.

'I shall be alright,' he said. 'A tenant made me angry.'

'Tell me what happened, and perhaps you will feel better.'

'Not tonight,' he said. 'The night will be spoilt by talking about him.'

Three

A succession of bills began reaching Mr Sufi's address: bills for clothing, liquor, cigars, petrol, household articles, furniture, billiard tables. At first he refused to believe that the purchases had been made by Gool and felt offended with the shopkeepers, assuming they were at fault. He rehearsed, again and again, what he would tell them: 'There is a mistake somewhere in your accounts department. This could lead to a loss of business prestige, you know.' He alternated between fits of rage and helplessness. Finally, in resignation, he sat down at his desk, wrote out cheques, addressed the envelopes, and went out to post them. At the post office he found more bills in his post box. It galled him that the bills were not temporary business phenomena but would come for as long as Gool lived. In order to replenish his plundered bank account — the Spider cost twice as much as his Jaguar — he increased the rent of his tenants. They objected. Some vacated their apartments immediately; others threatened to leave if he did not reconsider his decision. He remained adamant, saying that maintenance charges had risen.

He decided to 'divorce' his concubines. The decision was a painful one, but because of his changed relationship with Gool, he could no longer go on maintaining them, nor enjoying them. There was a night when, stretched out beside Abeda, he had been reminded by the bedside lamp of those other lamps — and, drained of all potency, he had risen and fled. To buttress his decision he reasoned that concubines were not rare jewels; he could dispose of them and keep them again when his former

13

life-pattern was restored. And should his concubines no longer be available, he would keep others. The bounty of Allah would always provide men with women. He felt glad that the bond between him and his concubines had been based on the barter system: he provided each one with an apartment and keep in exchange for erotic pleasure. He therefore had no scruples in ending the bond. Yet not wishing to forfeit his women totally (their presence on his premises would keep gossips quiet) he generously offered to let them stay on as tenants at lower rents. All except two left, fearing use without keep.

Both decisions — to increase the rent and 'divorce' his concubines — were largely determined by a surrender to fear and panic. The first brought him into conflict with his tenants, the second drove him into emotional isolation, forcing him to search within himself for resources to fend off Gool.

At the end of the month he waited as usual for Gool's visit, but Gool failed to arrive. Mr Sufi was bitterly disappointed. He wanted to enter the guests' room together with Gool to verify a belief that had fixed itself in his mind during the past week; the belief that the lamps did not exist. Lamps! Surely, he rationalised, they were part of the fairy world of Aladdin? Or an illusion woven by Gool? Perhaps he had begun to study magic and the creation of the lamps was a playful demonstration of his power. The strange and sudden manner in which things occurred that night — the prearranged telephone call, the arrival of five marionette-like helots with boxes on their shoulders, the seemingly infinite quantity of boxes, the conversion of his guests' room into a warehouse — pointed to the unreality of the lamps. If he entered the guests' room with the magician Gool, the truth of his belief would be vindicated.

For another reason he would have been happy to see Gool. By talking with his tormentor, or by virtue of his physical presence, Mr Sufi would find some comfort for his fractured being. But Gool was craftily keeping away. Since Gool had taken him under his 'protection', he had never, except last month, failed to pay his visit. Perhaps he was ill, or arrested, or killed? But he knew intuitively that these suppositions were idle: the man led a hero's life. And as the minutes passed, Gool's absence began to weigh on him and he yearned for the times when Gool unfailingly arrived to have tea with him.

Later that evening the bell rang. Mr Sufi hurried to the gate to welcome his belated visitor, but found two men who said they had brought five more boxes of lamps. Impaled with disappointment and the sudden collapse of his belief in the non-existence of the lamps, he allowed the men to leave the boxes on the balcony. When they left he told his wife to instruct the housemaids to store the lamps in the guests' room.

Mrs Zuleikha Sufi was a plump, fair-complexioned, grey-eyed woman, devoted to the rearing of her daughters and satisfying her husband's domestic needs. Considerate and kind, she gave away money to servants, children, beggars and charities. Over the years she had looked upon her husband's desire for other women as part of his manly privilege, sanctioned by religion, and though she had maintained no relationship with them, she had never hesitated to pay a clandestine visit to any of them if she learned of illness or death of a family member. She was grateful that her husband had never married any of his women or had children by them. Even the recent 'divorce' of his women she considered as falling within the ambit of his privilege. She neither questioned his motives nor regarded his action as something to be pleased over. Perhaps her husband felt that he was getting on in years and wished to stay at home and give her more children. If that was his intention, she was happy; she had always longed to give him a son. Now that he was home every night it would not be long before she fell pregnant.

Zuleikha soon learned that her husband was no longer the same man whose quiet presence had once ruled her life. He was subject to starts and depressions, he found fault with the food, was irritated by talk, by the tinkle of cutlery. She was afraid to question him. She had noticed these changes since the night the lamps had arrived, but she felt it would be impertinent to tread into a man's world by asking questions. She went about her household duties quietly, trying to please him in every way she could. Even when, unable to unburden himself to her, he relegated her to another bedroom, she accepted it calmly, unlike a wife who had always shared her husband's bed.

Emir Sufi's relationship with his family had always been a loose one. Preoccupied with his pleasures outside the home and his role as a landlord, he had relinquished his family to the periphery of his life. He had fathered four girls and their rearing was left to his wife. He thought that providing them with the usual necessities of life was his principal duty. He was a stranger to the joys of playing with his children, of taking delight in their beauty and innocence, even of spoiling them with over-indulgence. In fact, the birth of the girls had been a sharp disappointment to him. He felt that his wife, by not producing boys, had diminished his masculine status and reduced his image in society. But that was not all. The girls were also liabilities: eventually they would be the instruments of the dispersal of his wealth; and more, the extinction of his name. Consequently, his daughters had not been given the love and devotion of a father.

The arrival of five more boxes of lamps shook Mr Sufi: they were a reality that implicated him criminally. He felt outraged. He went downstairs and climbed into his Jaguar.

He drove about the streets aimlessly, but shunned the neon-lit area of the cinemas and the gay crowds. Then he steered his car through quiet streets in search of solace. He passed through Park Road, turned into Lovers' Walk, Avenue Road, Lilian Road, Park Road again. Then he drove to Crown Road.

He parked his car in a pool of shadow under a plane tree and rested his head on the steering wheel. Where could he find solace? He thought of the mosque. He drove to the one in Newtown; when he reached it the muezzin's call for prayers erupted from the minaret. He parked his car, but remained seated, immobilised by indecision. He had never attended evening prayers at the mosque (having confined himself to the formality of attending noon prayers on Fridays) and the small devout congregation would be startled to see him. They would guess that a troubled mind had driven him there. Several men in black cloaks and white skull-caps passed along the pavement and he watched them until they disappeared through the gates of the mosque. He started his car and drove to the Lyric cinema.

He entered the cinema without looking at the posters and without the usual box of chocolates in his hand. The film turned out to be Bergman's 'The Virgin Spring'. The evil atmosphere of the film terrified him and he fled.

He drove about the streets again. When he passed 'Kashmiri Flats' he stopped. His friend Abu-salaam, who owned the building, lived there. It occurred to him that perhaps Gool had also given

16

Abu-salaam some lamps. In fact Gool might have given lamps to all the landlords under his 'protection'. If he knew this he would have the consolation of being involved with others. He parked his car and hurried up the stairs, but he stopped when he saw the stairs illuminated. He looked up at the lamp as though he had seen it for the first time. His eyes filmed with tears and the lamp seemed to splinter.

Abu-salaam was about to have tea and was happy to see his friend. He was in his dressing-gown and looked very relaxed.

'How are you Emir? I haven't seen you for some time.'

'I was passing by and thought of visiting you before going home,' Mr Sufi explained.

'It's not time for bed yet, but I relax better in my night clothes,' Abu-salaam said, handing Mr Sufi a cup of tea.

'How's business getting on?' Mr Sufi asked.

'A little slack for this time of the year, but one can't make money all the time,' he answered, relishing his tea. Abu-salaam owned a clothing factory.

Mr Sufi found himself overwhelmed with envy of the man. He looked so blithely contented that he could not help saying:

'I shall send you several boxes of lamps tomorrow.'

'Lamps?'

'Yes, I obtained some very cheaply at a sale.'

'Thank you, but I have enough in stock to last a long time.'

Elation filled Mr Sufi. His friend could only have received them from Gool. He eagerly waited for him to confess. But Abu-salaam went on sipping tea.

'I am giving you the lamps free.'

'Why do you want to give them away? You have so many flats to see to and your stairs always seem to be without lights.'

A squall of acrimony and discord beat within Mr Sufi. Not only was there an accusing reference to his stairs, but his charitable overture was spurned. For a moment even his vision was affected and Abu-salaam appeared physically distorted. Enmity welled up within him and he struggled desperately to curb the words that spilled from his lips:

'Has Gool given you lamps?'

'Gool given me lamps? What a curious thing to say. Did he give you the lamps?'

'No,' he said, hastily swallowing the tea and rising from the arm-chair.

'Where are you going? I'm just beginning to enjoy myself.'
'I must go,' he stammered and left hurriedly.

Four

As the days passed Mr Sufi sought refuge in cinemas from his inner torment and constant preoccupation with himself. Cocooned within a crepuscular world, he felt safe while watching comedies, adventures (ancient and modern), love stories and science fiction. He shunned films whose titles suggested personal suffering. Of course there was always the danger of running into Gool. But he made certain of not meeting him by circling the cinema in his car first to establish that Gool's Spider was not in the vicinity.

One Friday evening Mr Sufi went to the Avalon cinema. While he was examining the posters outside, Riad, one of his tenants, came up to him and said:

'How are you Mr Sufi? Would you like to come in?'

'Are they showing a comedy?'

'No. We are having a live show. There are some beautiful girls on stage.'

Mr Sufi went towards the ticket office.

'No, you don't have to pay. Come with me.'

And he led him towards the entrance door and into the foyer.

'Are you the new manager here?' Mr Sufi asked.

'No. But let me introduce you to some friends first,' Riad said as they approached several men.

Riad introduced them to Mr Sufi, and then had an idea.

'I think I will introduce Mr Sufi to the audience and give him the honour of crowning Miss Venus and awarding the trophies.'

Mr Sufi was puzzled but Riad went on to explain:

'We are all members of the Spartan Gymnasium. We are having

our annual contest, but this time we have also arranged a stage show. Come inside and have a look.'

Riad led Mr Sufi up the stairs and they emerged into the heart of the auditorium. They were ushered to seats.

A blues singer was singing into a microphone in her hand. As she swayed she revealed long legs through a black satin dress slit down the sides. The band played at the foot of the stage.

When she had done the audience applauded. She sang another song and Mr Sufi began to feel at ease and looked forward to enjoying himself.

The next item was a dance called 'The Cat Walk' performed by a man and a woman and suggestive of a furtive love encounter. Then followed an acrobatic display, a judo demonstration, a eurhythmics performance and finally several rousing folk songs from the Cape.

Then a banner was brought on stage and pinned to the rear curtains. The banner read: 'Miss Venus Contest'.

'You are going to enjoy this,' Riad said.

Martial music resounded and simultaneously a bevy of bikini-clad women marched on to the stage. Mr Sufi found his whole body in delightful effervescence at the sight of the lovely array of female flesh, ranging from the sheen of ebony to porcelain white.

'Have a closer look, Mr Sufi,' Riad said, and handed him a pair of opera glasses.

He raised the glasses to his eyes and gave a sudden start as the women plunged across his vision. They walked across the stage, their limbs moving in unison, their arms gently swaying, their heads held erect. Then they assembled for everyone to admire and applaud them. The curtains were drawn and when they re-opened a beam of light revealed the single figure of a woman. She smiled, turned, walked several steps, looked at the judges below her in the front seats, then walked smartly away, the light pursuing her. The spectators applauded and there was some whistling by men. Another woman entered and the display went on. Fifteen women had entered for the contest and Mr Sufi kept his connoisseur's eye fixed on them, his entire body braced by the spectacle.

When the last contestant left the stage Riad said:

'Come, you must crown our Miss Venus.'

'No. Some other time.'

'It will only take a second. I will stand beside you. Please come.'

Mr Sufi's refusal had been uttered out of politeness and a wish not to dislocate prior arrangements, but when Riad insisted he agreed, as the opportunity of crowning a beautiful woman might not come to him again.

The two men mounted the stage, in the middle of which a tinsel-decorated throne now stood. A judge passed to Riad a slip of paper on which was written the name of the winner. Riad announced her name. Miss Venus entered and Riad placed a scarlet cloak over her shoulders and handed her a staff. She sat down on the throne. Mr Sufi found a crown of artificial jewels thrust into his hand and he went up to Miss Venus and crowned her. Music and applause proclaimed the coronation of Miss Venus and cameras flashed on all sides. Then all the other contestants came on stage and Mr Sufi found himself corralled by a bevy of gorgeous women.

Suddenly all the lights were switched on and the stage was crowded by members of the audience, congratulating Miss Venus. Mr Sufi was rudely pushed aside. He found himself at the rear of the stage, an insignificant figure banished by a jubilant horde. Riad looked for him, found him at last, and took him by the arm.

'Come, let us return to our seats.'

Soon everyone left the stage and another banner was brought which read: 'Mr Apollo Contest'. This banner was pinned over the first banner.

The word Apollo reverberated painfully within Mr Sufi; and he thought of fleeing. But he had already enjoyed so much of the show without having paid that he felt it would be discourteous to leave. Besides, the entrance door might be closed and he might find himself trapped in the foyer. The lights on the stage were now extinguished and the banner was in shadow. Then a disc of light illuminated the front of the stage.

A contestant appeared in the disc and began to display the muscles of his body. When he had finished he was greeted with a burst of applause.

'He is one of the finalists,' Riad said. 'We had the elimination contest at the gymnasium yesterday. Two more and then the winner will be selected.'

The next contestant appeared and he went through the same ritual of muscle display. Then the third one came on. He seemed to be the favourite to win as he was greeted with loud applause.

21

When he had gone all the lights were switched on and the word Apollo seared Mr Sufi's eyes.

'Come,' Riad said. 'You must award the trophy to the winner.'

'No,' Mr Sufi protested.

'Come. Afterwards you can meet Miss Venus.'

He accompanied Riad as though impelled by some mechanism within him. Everyone applauded the two men as they ascended the stage. Riad addressed the audience.

'Ladies and gentlemen, in a few minutes I will announce the winner of the Mr Apollo contest. In the meantime, I want to introduce to you a patron of the Spartan Gymnasium, Mr Sufi. He is not only a well-known man, but a man who has shown the keenest interest in the perfection of the human body, in health, strength and beauty which are our mottoes ... '

Mr Sufi, a short corpulent figure in the glare of the stage lights, failed to discern the hundreds of faces in the dim auditorium looking at him ironically. All he saw was a cinematographic blur.

' ... in what we all have in common, whether rich or poor, learned or ignorant ... '

One of the judges came forward to the foot of the stage and handed to Riad a slip of paper. At the same time the three contestants entered and Riad signalled to one of them to stand on a small wooden dais, and to the other two to flank him.

'Ladies and gentlemen, I take pleasure in announcing the winner of our Mr Apollo Contest, Brutus Gabo.'

Mr Sufi found a large trophy in his hand and he went forward to give it to the winner. Mr Apollo took the trophy and shook Mr Sufi's hand. Mr Sufi winced at the pain of crushed fingers while camera flashlights attacked him from all directions. There was loud applause, but some men in the front rows, perceiving the physical variance between the two men, burst into laughter. He heard this mocking under-current of merriment and felt a gust of profound loneliness, misery and insignificance of being sweep through him among all those people.

As during the Miss Venus Contest he found himself pushed to the rear of the stage by a crowd and it was while he was trying to recover from his ordeal that Riad took him by the arm.

'Come, you can meet Miss Venus now.'

Riad led him to a glass-panelled office in the foyer of the cinema.

'Sit down, Mr Sufi. She will be here in a few minutes. Tomorrow

22

you can come to the gymnasium and take her out for a drive. She is not a difficult girl . . . '

After a while three men entered and shook Mr Sufi's hand, one of them again sadistically crushing his fingers.

'I am Apollo,' Brutus said, seeing that Mr Sufi failed to recognise him. In his suit he did not look as big as he had appeared on the stage where the light had accentuated his muscle contours. The other two men were the defeated contestants, Julius and Anthony.

The crowd leaving the cinema was beginning to thin. Then Mr Sufi saw Miss Venus approaching. She still wore her crown and cloak. She was accompanied by two women still in their bikinis and by the men he had met in the foyer when he arrived.

Miss Venus and the other two women were introduced by Riad to Mr Sufi. Miss Venus kissed Mr Sufi and sat down on a chair beside him. Riad addressed him:

'Mr Sufi, we have been honoured by your presence and I want to express, on behalf of the members of the Spartan Gymnasium, our gratitude. As a patron, you will appreciate . . . (Miss Venus stretched out her hand and placed it gently on Mr Sufi's lap) . . . that there are the usual expenses in holding contests, not to mention the requirements of our gymnasium — and that a donation will be highly appreciated.'

Mr Sufi took out his cheque book, wrote out a page and handed it to Riad.

Riad smiled. Miss Venus withdrew her hand. Everyone thanked Mr Sufi and took leave, Mr Apollo once again using the opportunity to crush his fingers. He was left alone with Riad. Riad escorted him out of the office to the cinema door.

'Good night, Mr Sufi. I have some clearing up to do.'

Riad shut the door behind him.

Mr Sufi stood on the pavement beside his car for a while, a lonely figure in the feeble light of a street lamp outside the deserted cinema.

Five

The conviction that Gool had given lamps to all the landlords under his protection took hold of Mr Sufi's mind. There was no reason for Gool to give them to him only. He was surely aware of the advantage of distributing the lamps to all. If only he could establish his belief he would have the consolation of being part of a group. Should the police start investigating he would not be the only one to be implicated. But there was an abyss for him to cross. None of those who enjoyed Gool's protection ever spoke of it; nor did they enquire of another, nor confess to another, of any dealings with him. There was a tacit contract to remain silent. But it was vital for his mind's peace that he establish his belief and in this only Abu-salaam could help him. Had he not mentioned that he had enough lamps in store to last for a long time?

Mr Sufi visited Abu-salaam again. He had no clear idea how he would elicit the information. He hoped that at some point in the conversation he would be able to ambush Abu-salaam and get a confession from him; or that Abu-salaam would inadvertently say something that would constitute clear proof; or that a jest would contain the kernel of an admission. He called upon his friend at about the same time as on the previous occasion, hoping to find him in the same relaxed mood.

When he knocked on the door, Abu-salaam's wife opened it.

'Abu is in the bathroom, but he should be out in a minute. Sit down.'

He sat in an armchair and waited, but his friend seemed to be in no hurry to come out of the bathroom. He smoked several cigarettes and was a little surprised that Abu-salaam's wife did not come to keep him company. She seemed to have disappeared as he did not hear her moving about.

When at last Abu-salaam appeared in his bathrobe, looking flushed, Mr Sufi said:

'I may be going to Durban next weekend. Do you want to come?'

'Why should I?'

There was something curt about the question, but he decided to ignore it.

'It isn't pleasant going alone on a long journey,' Mr Sufi said.

'I shall never go with you!' Abu-salaam said, sitting down on the edge of a settee with his elbows on his knees and looking scornfully at Mr Sufi.

'I thought . . . ' Mr Sufi began in a tremulous voice.

'You thought many things! Tell me what you meant the other night when you asked if Gool had given me some lamps?'

A pulse of joy passed through Mr Sufi. So the man had received some lamps from Gool!

'I didn't mean . . . ' he protested gently.

'You didn't mean? What! Weren't you trying to suggest that I was receiving certain supplies in my factory . . .? What were you trying to find out?'

Mr Sufi felt a frigid gust sweep through some void within him. He realised that Abu-salaam had commercial dealings with Gool and had not received any lamps.

Pointing an accusing finger at Mr Sufi, Abu-salaam went on:

'You will soon go and tell everyone . . . of my private business affairs. Why can't you keep your mouth shut and not talk of things that should not be mentioned . . . You . . . '

'Why don't you hit him!' a voice screeched near Mr Sufi. He saw an apparition in a green dress.

A horde of words from Abu-salaam ambushed and attacked him.

'Just what did you mean? You think I don't know you were trying to get me involved . . . Even now coming at night . . . trying to take me to Durban . . . Why did you come then looking so upset . . . You were trying . . . '

Unable to answer, cowering in his armchair, his vision captive to hallucination, Mr Sufi looked at the woman near him for help and to his horror saw her undergoing a demon transformation.

'Hit him!' she screeched again.

A furious green-winged harpy swooped upon him.

He found himself in the street, his body miraculously intact. He recalled the aggressive harpy, and a warrior who desperately tried to fend her away from him, at the same time pushing him towards the door which he was unable to see.

Six

After several months had passed Gool telephoned Mr Sufi.

'I am coming to fetch you in a few minutes' time. Some friends of mine want to meet you.'

As soon as he put the telephone down fears began to rack him. He was now going to appear in public with the gangster. His involvement with Gool was to become more firmly spliced. Perhaps he would introduce him to men who were wicked, more ruthlessly demanding. He waited for Gool on the balcony like a prisoner, restlessly pacing up to the gate and retreating to the furthest end. He desperately hoped that something would prevent Gool from reaching him, a collision with a bus or a sudden fissure in the road. But Gool came. Feeling numb, he accompanied him down the stairs. The sports car was parked in the street and a group of people were standing beside it, admiring it. Mr Sufi hesitated.

'Let's go in my Jaguar.'

'It's too hot in a closed car.'

Gool opened the door of the Spider for Mr Sufi. He climbed in without daring to look around and see whose eyes were focused upon him. Gool got in, started the Spider and drove off at speed.

'You must have missed me,' Gool said, smiling. 'I was away in Durban.'

'Yes,' he answered feebly, his mouth filling with a blast of air that painfully distended his gullet for a second. Then he was seized by the illusion of the streets, the buildings, the lamp-posts receding on a swift noisy conveyor belt while he sat in a stationary

27

car, and was therefore not surprised when Gool's premises in High Road came to a halt beside him.

Gool opened the car's door and they went inside. There were several policemen in uniform seated around the table, drinking liquor.

'Gentlemen, meet my friend Mr Sufi. He owns half of Fordsburg.'

The policemen rose from their seats and shook hands.

'Brandy,' Gool said, handing Mr Sufi a glass. He took it mechanically.

'Mr Sufi, if you are ever in trouble, these friends will stand by you.'

They all drank to Mr Sufi's health and happiness and bit into oriental dainties.

'You are not drinking, Mr Sufi,' Gool reminded him. 'Would you prefer wine?'

Mr Sufi took the liquor at one gulp, and then began to cough violently. Gool offered him his handkerchief and poured more liquor into his glass.

'You must sip the liquor,' Gool advised him.

The policemen were thirsty and drank without restraint. One of them quipped that dealing with crime was a 'thirsty business', and Mr Sufi was surprised to hear himself say that 'some people have a thirst for crime', at which Gool laughed uproariously and slapped Mr Sufi's back with gusto.

'We are all in business together,' Gool said. 'You collect rent, I collect fees and they collect fines.'

Everyone laughed, except Mr Sufi who saw no connection in their respective vocations in life.

'But there is a difference,' Gool went on, addressing his ward.

'You receive, I pay. There are the boys, their families, the lawyers — and let us not forget our friends here.'

'Yes, yes,' Gool's friends chorused.

After some further drinking and eating, Gool took them all to look at his premises. He showed them the expensive new furniture he had recently acquired. Then he invited everyone to the billiard room. Several men were engaged in playing, but when the party arrived they laid down their billiard sticks and stood aside.

'Gentlemen,' Gool addressed everyone, standing beside Mr Sufi with his hand on his shoulder, 'Mr Sufi donated this new billiard table to our club.' He clapped his hands and everyone clapped as well. 'On behalf of all I thank him. And I take this opportunity to say that we shall stand by him through thick and thin.'

They all applauded.

'Let me play a game with you,' Gool said to Mr Sufi.

'I am not used to this,' Mr Sufi protested, feeling unsteady on his legs. Gool led him to the edge of the table while Akbar gathered the balls. One of the men offered them two cues.

'Mr Sufi, you must hit the ivory ball with the stick,' Gool said.

Mr Sufi looked at the ball — which tantalisingly divided itself cell-wise into twins — bent over the table, drew the billiard cue back and thrust it at the target. The cue failed to touch the ball and everyone laughed.

'That will do,' Gool said, coming to his rescue. Everyone fell silent. Gool took his position at the table and bent over, telling Mr Sufi to stand behind him and hold the end of the cue. Mr Sufi obliged and Gool smacked the ivory ball straight into the grouped balls. They fled to the edges of the table.

Everyone applauded.

The policemen decided to leave and Gool and Mr Sufi went outside with them to say good-bye.

'I think you need some freshening up,' Gool said to Mr Sufi after the policemen had gone. 'Let's go for a drive.'

As the sports car wove through the streets Mr Sufi felt that shocked and disapproving eyes were observing him as he sat beside a notorious criminal. When Gool stopped outside Broadway Cinema and said, 'I want to get a few tickets for this evening,' he felt even more exposed. It was about time for the matinée show to be over. His fear was abruptly realised. The doors of the cinema opened and people came flocking out. Several men recognised him and greeted him. In desperation he looked for the gadget in the car that operated the hood, but failed to find it. Gool returned, but stood beside the Spider and talked to several people. They looked at Mr Sufi. Then Gool got in and drove away.

The car flashed across a highway straddling the city and Mr Sufi began to panic. For the first time he conceived the possibility that Gool might kill him. He might drive him to some lonely spot in the country and there enact one of those gruesome crimes he had seen on cinema screens.

Gool drove to the Zoo Lake. He parked the car under some willows. Before them spread an idyllic view: a mirror of water on which boats and ducks were gliding. Gool lit two cigarettes and gave Mr Sufi one.

'Mr Sufi, you know you owe me a cheque.'

He produced his cheque book from his pocket.

'Here's a pen,' Gool said. 'But you will have difficulty in writing it out. Let me help you.'

He handed Gool the cheque book.

'I hope you don't mind; I am adding two little zeros to the usual sum. You know how many payments I have to make.'

Mr Sufi, beginning to feel restful after the panic that had seized him earlier, did not object. The placidness of the lake-scene added to his feeling of rest and he saw no reason to agitate himself because Gool wished to add two little zeros. In fact he felt grateful to Gool for graciously sparing his life.

Gool returned the cheque book to Mr Sufi and got out of the car.

'Come, let us get a boat.'

Mr Sufi went with him to the boathouse where Gool hired a boat from an attendant. He jumped into the boat and taking the oars asked Mr Sufi to join him. He hesitated. A clot of words declining the invitation stuck in his throat.

'Hold the oar and jump in.'

Gool held out an oar to him, but Mr Sufi decided to clamber into the boat unaided.

They glided swiftly over the lake, ducks and swans flapping their wings frantically to get out of the way. There was an islet in the middle of the lake and the boat cut towards it, past other boats loaded with gay young men and women. A vapour, faintly smelling of rotted lake plants, rose from the surface of the lake and Mr Sufi saw within its depths a muddy night. A thrill of fear pulsed through him.

'It's lovely, isn't it?' Gool said, holding the oars above water for a few seconds.

'Yes,' he answered, involuntarily dipping his hand into the lake. The rush of the cool water filled him with dizziness.

The boat reached the shore of the islet and seemed to Mr Sufi to have been stopped by some unheard lake's fiat from below. And to his amazement, the islet, with its willows, acacias, flowering shrubs and variety of bird life began to circle on its own axis. He sat petrified, clutching the plank of his seat. Suddenly a gale seemed to blow into his face dispelling the hallucination and the boat's prow raced towards the boathouse.

Gool jumped out of the boat as it reached the landing-stage near the boathouse and held out his hand to his passenger, who took it gratefully and climbed out.

'That was lovely,' Gool said, breathing in deeply and flexing his arms. 'Let us take a walk now.'

They walked along the lake's margin, the western sun flaming low down in the sky. Gool pointed at some waterfowl among reeds and then, kneeling on a flat rock near the bank, drew Mr Sufi's attention to tiny yellow fish. They walked on and stopped on a small bridge that crossed a rivulet flowing into the lake. A large fish broke the calm waters, and they watched the expanding water rings until they disappeared.

'Beautiful. That's nature,' Gool said.

They neared some oaks. (These were the same trees near which Mr Sufi had parked his car many nights ago, his heart filled with a longing to confide in Olga sitting beside him.) As they reached the oaks loud raucous cries — like barbaric laughter — erupted. Several hadeda ibises rushed into the orange and red sky. Mr Sufi was shocked. The cries seemed to herald an attack on him by Gool. Darkness covered his eyes as he looked up at the trees. He felt himself losing his grip on life.

'They are loud, aren't they?' Gool said.

He heard Gool's voice in the distance, as though through a tunnel.

Gool had moved away from under the oaks to watch the flight of the birds. He shaded his eyes with his hand and watched them fly away towards the sun's flaming corolla and melt into gold. He then returned to Mr Sufi who was recovering from the shock.

'These trees are very old,' Gool said. 'Sometimes I wish I was a tree. Then the older I'd grow the deeper my roots would sink into the earth.'

'Yes,' Mr Sufi said, feeling inspired by Gool's appreciation of the oaks. 'They are beautiful.'

And he touched the trunk of a tree and felt the rough strong bark. Gool's implied confession of human frailty restored within him the tranquillity that had been so sharply fractured by the ibises.

'We must go home now,' Gool said, and they returned to the car.

When Gool's Spider stormed into Fordsburg it was dusk.

In the sanctuary of his home Mr Sufi was filled with elation. He considered it a miracle that he could still be alive after being alone with Gool. His elation extended into the evening and he was gripped by an expansive, charitable mood. He went downstairs to Mr Das Patel's café on the ground floor of 'Orient Mansions' and, sitting down on a chair which the café-owner hastily provided began to talk animatedly with several people lounging there. Mr Das Patel plied his landlord with refreshments.

'Mr Das Patel,' Mr Sufi said, 'give everyone here some refreshments and a box of 'Black Magic' chocolates . . . at my expense.'

The café-owner went around offering refreshments and chocolates. Several schoolboys entered and Mr Sufi told him to provide for them too.

'Never neglect students, Mr Das Patel. They are our bright stars.'

Mr Sufi sipped a fruit drink. Everyone was surprised at his transformed personality. They had never seen him in a convivial, generous mood before.

'By the way, boys,' Mr Das Patel said, 'Yogi Krishnasiva he come out of prison soon.'

'When?' several voices wanted to know.

'Let me see.' He went to a calendar hanging on one side of a glass case full of cakes. 'I count every day since he go jail, but I make sure now.' He turned the pages of the calendar.

The Yogi was a very well-known man who lived on the second floor of 'Orient Mansions'. About a year before he had been arrested under the Immorality Act for making love to a white woman. He had been tried and imprisoned.

'In six weeks exact,' Mr Das Patel said, coming from behind the counter. 'Dey make him real yogi in jail, boys. Hard bread and water. He not get white cake dere!'

Everyone laughed at the innuendo.

'Tell me, boys,' Mr Sufi said, 'I have been puzzled by the meaning of the name Gool. You are educated. You should know.'

'You should ask Gool,' one of them said, but Mr Sufi answered stiffly: 'It is not a joking matter. My enquiry is connected with no one. Do you know the meaning of your own name, whatever it is?'

The boy thought it best to shake his head.

'Gool means rose in Persian,' another ventured.

'Fancy calling a man a rose!'

Everyone laughed.

Mr Sufi, taking delight in his schoolmasterish role, began to question the boys again but they seemed ignorant of the meaning of the word. Then one of them who had been thoughtful for some time shouted:

'I've got it! Gool is an Arabic word for an evil spirit preying on corpses. One reads about them in Eastern stories.'

Mr Sufi's hand, holding a bottle of fruit drink, trembled, and his face flushed.

'No!' he shouted. 'You are being stupid!'

The boy looked ashamed and Mr Sufi, supported by his anger, was able to regain control of himself.

'Must I tell you the meaning of the word? It is short for "goolam" and you should know the meaning of that word.'

'Slave,' the boy said hesitantly.

'Yes, slave,' he said laughing, forgiving the boy and forgetting the 'ghoul' of Eastern stories.

'Yes, isn't it curious. And does any one of you know why a name like that should be given to a son? Because of the superstitious belief that it would keep away evil invoked by the envious.'

And he laughed again in an unusual hysteria-tainted voice.

That night as he climbed the stairs of 'Orient Mansions' the words 'slave' and 'Gool' seemed to drum rhythmically in his brain with every step he took. He stopped on the dark stairs, pondering on the significance of the singular irony that a man named slave was the master of his life. Was it the deliberate intent of some mischievous force to bewilder and poison his reason? In a rational world a man such as Gool could not exist. Perhaps he was an agent or embodiment of some occult evil . . . Yes . . . there he was standing on the second floor landing, surrounded by a livid aura . . . He was coming down towards him step by step . . . He was a ghoul!

The demon sprang upon him and was grappling with him, while explosions of raucous laughter erupted from demented lips.

He fell on the steps and awoke from his nightmarish hallucination, his ears still ringing with reverberating laughter. Fear seized him as he lay on the cold steps, until, gathering some superhuman energy within him, he rose and rushed up the stairs. When he reached the top floor landing his wife and Fawzia were at the gate.

'There was someone,' he said, trembling.

'We heard laughter,' his wife said, opening the gate and quickly locking it after her husband had entered.

Several people from the second floor came hurriedly to the gate with torches and enquired if anything was wrong. They had heard horrible laughter.

'There was a madman,' Mr Sufi said, trying to regain his self-possession.

'I saw him going down . . . '

'Saw?'

'Well . . . there is some light from the stair-window.'

'Did he try to harm you?'

'No . . . I am alright . . . Goodnight.'

Mr Sufi went to lie down in his bedroom while his wife prepared some tea for him. In the illuminated, comforting atmosphere of his bedroom he soon forgot the experience on the dark stairs. The overwhelming fact that he was alive prevented him from probing into the nature of his experience and filled him with a rising euphoria so that when his wife brought his tea he said he would have some cake as well.

While having tea and cake it occurred to him that he was now presented with the opportunity to have the stairs lit — the madman would be his excuse — without having to succumb to humiliating pressure from tenants. Since Gool had given him the lamps he had on several occasions tilted with himself, but had not found the courage to have the stairs lit. The practice of saving on the cost of electricity had become a sort of fetish with him. He had also feared that lighting the stairs could lead to his arrest. For instance, a tenant might learn that lamps had been stolen from some warehouse or factory and link the theft with the sudden illumination of the stairs. But, he reflected, the lit stairs of 'Orient Mansions' would not set a precedent. He would never agree to any request by tenants in his other buildings to have stairs lit.

Next morning he took six lamps from a cupboard in his office and told one of the housemaids to attach them to the light-fittings along the stair walls. The lamps in his guests' room he would never use.

Seven

For weeks Zuleikha Sufi had been preparing to attend the wedding of a relative in a distant country town. She had been to the dressmaker who had meticulously sewn the dresses for herself and her daughters. Fawzia was the eldest. She was eighteen years old, very elegant, with plaited thick black hair that usually fell over her right shoulder. Her face was serenely beautiful with dark eyes flashing beneath sleek eyelashes and kohl-blackened eyelids. Salma, the second eldest, was twelve years old. She looked like a dusky Egyptian. Then came Nazreena who was four years old and Ruwayda who was three: they looked so much alike with large glaucous eyes and brown hair that one could mistake them for twins.

Fawzia was to be a bridesmaid and her dress had been sewn according to specifications. Mrs Sufi had visited many shops before purchasing the gifts for the bride and bridegroom; gifts that had stirred her girls into a flurry of excitement as they were given the task of wrapping them and tying them with coloured ribbons. In fact for Fawzia it was a special occasion: it was at weddings that men who wished to marry scrutinised young women and marriage proposals often came soon afterwards.

So for Mrs Sufi the wedding was not only a festive time, with her husband joining the family— something he rarely did otherwise — but an event that could lead to Fawzia's marriage. She wanted her daughters to look beautiful, as indeed they were, and she sent them a day before to the hairdresser's to have their hair elaborately curled and perfumed. And she had her own hair attended to by the hairdresser at home.

On the morning of the wedding day Zuleikha and her daughters rose at an early hour and dressed themselves. Her husband was up also; he was in the bathroom, and though she felt some anxiety about his health (there were days when he did not look well) she refrained from asking him if he was well enough to take them in the car. She would have been able to bear the disappointment of not attending the wedding: not so her daughters. But her anxiety about his health dissipated when he came to breakfast dressed in his new suit, especially ordered from the tailor for the occasion, and looking fit.

Mother and daughters happily went down to the basement where the cars were parked and Mr Sufi followed them after locking the gate. He was going to take his family in the new Mercedes which he had recently bought and, anticipating that a great deal of talk would centre on the car, he felt something of the delight weddings had always given him.

On the way Mr Sufi's thoughts began to wander from the delights of the wedding. By now everyone must have heard of his changed life and of his new companion. Among the guests there would certainly be people from Johannesburg and they would spread the news, if they saw him, to others. In fact, they would say, they had recently seen him with Gool riding brazenly in the Spider through the city streets. Slowly panic began to swell in him, and the car which had sped along swiftly began to decelerate gradually. His wife and daughters were unaware of the tumult in his mind as they were used to his reserve. Yes, talk about the Mercedes might lead to talk about the expensive Spider he had bought for Gool. Others might even daringly say that he had been forced to 'divorce' his concubines as Gool and his gang had ravished them.

Disturbed by these reflections, Mr Sufi became the prey of wilder imaginings. Thieves might break into his residence while he was enjoying himself at the wedding and mischievously decide to telephone the police and inform them of the lamps stored in his guests' room. He could not . . . He suddenly swung the car off the road and stopped under a tree. He placed his hands on the steering wheel and rested his head on them with a sigh.

'What's the matter?' his wife cried, alarmed.

'I am not feeling well.'

'We must get home quickly.'

'The wedding!' Fawzia cried.

'Fawzia!' her mother said angrily, looking back. She saw the disappointed faces of her daughters.

'I am sorry, mummy,' Fawzia said penitently.

Zuleikha saw a house along the roadside. They were about thirty miles away from the city.

'Let me go and get help,' she said, opening the door of the car.

'No, don't go,' her husband said feebly.

'Perhaps there is someone who could help by driving us home.'

'I will manage,' Mr Sufi said. He started the car and turned it in the direction of home.

Zuleikha watched her husband with anxiety. She remembered his experience on the stairs and regretted her selfishness in not having asked him in the morning if he was well enough to take them. Her daughters sat silently, tears welling in their eyes. Although concerned about their father, they could not banish the disappointment they felt in not going to the wedding: days of joyous preparation and expectation came to nothing in an instant.

Only when Mr Sufi reached home did the disappointment he had caused his wife and children register in his consciousness. He felt wretched.

Zuleikha helped her husband to bed and, despite his protest that his illness was temporary, telephoned the doctor. She also telephoned her relatives and told them they would not attend the wedding.

The doctor found nothing physically wrong with his patient, but did not say so. He prescribed some sedatives.

Eight

When Mr Sufi came to hear of Yogi Krishnasiva's release from prison, he decided to pay him a commiserative visit. The Yogi had always been a model tenant and though many people had derived amusement from his fall — especially politicians who despised him for declaring that if one possessed inner liberty political liberty was unnecessary — he had felt sorry for him for he too was strongly attracted to women. But there was another reason why he wished to visit him. He felt that the Yogi's theoretical insight into the instability of life had gained a practical dimension by his penal experience and that he was now a much wiser man. If he were able to confide in the Yogi regarding his own problem, he would certainly receive advice that would help him.

The Yogi's mother opened the door. She was a bulbous woman whose flowing sari's heroic attempt to conceal her shape failed around her midriff where the flesh came out in rolls.

'Thank you for coming to see my son. You know what people are. They all hate him. Sit down.'

'I want to speak to him.'

'He has changed.'

'Changed?'

'Yes, he won't speak to anyone. And he has given up walking.'

'Given up . . . '

'Come and see.'

He followed her. She opened a door, let him in and closed it. The curtains were drawn and the room was faintly lit by a flame-bud burning on an altar-table in a clay bowl before a brass figurine of the dancing god Shiva. Several incense sticks bloomed and smoked from a small porcelain vase.

He looked for the Yogi but saw no form seated in the usual meditation posture. Scanning the room, he saw what looked like two upright cobras — as though some petulant charmer had transfixed them. His eyes followed the length of the cobras to the floor and there he saw two eyes staring at him. He sat down on the carpet and looked at the Yogi, convinced that as soon as he recognised his landlord he would bring his feet down. But the Yogi remained poised on his head. To assist the Yogi into recognition he every now and then tilted his head and when that failed resorted to chanting his name several times, mantra-wise.

He realised that he would have to be patient. The Yogi could not remain in an inverted position for ever. While waiting he reflected on some of the beliefs that were part of the ascetic way of life. There was the belief that life was an illusion. Why was this so when everything pointed to its reality? If he accepted this axiom, then by the necessity of logic, he would have to regard Gool as a dream figure and all his fears as groundless. But the Yogi's fall demonstrated the falsity of the belief; he had tried to deny the reality of life and life had caught up with him. There was also the belief that the souls of men entered into beasts and birds. If he had a choice he would have liked to be a bird, preferably a falcon, for then he would have sway over two kingdoms, the terrestrial and the ethereal. Was reincarnation and its related doctrine of karma possible? Could he have been a gangster in a previous life and was he therefore in this life, by the demands of retributive justice, condemned to experience the pangs of a victim? But there was a fatal flaw in this belief, for how could one expiate meaningfully if one had no idea of the wrong perpetrated in a previous incarnation? Or was suffering just a case of occult mischief?

They came upon him unexpectedly, two horrid cobras that locked themselves in a pincer-grip around his neck. He tried to rise — out of a nightmare — shouted mutely for help, dragged them across the floor, gasped, moaned, and fell against the door. That saved him.

The Yogi's mother opened the door and threw herself on the two men. She eventually succeeded in freeing her landlord's neck

from her son's coiled feet. Mr Sufi, thankful, hurried out of the
room without hearing her apologies.

Nine

One day Mr Sufi went to collect rent from a Mr Rahim who was consistently late in his payments. When he presented himself at his door, Mr Rahim in an irate mood said:

'Are you not rich enough? Must you increase the rent?'

His words seemed to be a prearranged signal, for immediately he uttered them several doors were flung open and Mr Sufi found himself surrounded by a host of tenants and their children.

Mr Sufi, though he abhorred tenants who made him wait for long periods or tried to evade payment, had always been delighted that there were a few tenants such as Mr Rahim who never paid their rents when due, for it gave him the opportunity to visit them. He had found Mr Rahim — a small, wiry, lean-faced man with brown, restless, protruding eyes — a delightful fellow and had always marvelled at his ability to devise plausible excuses for not paying on time. He would open the door and hobble on one leg, moaning with pain; or appear with his neck swathed in bandages; or emerge from an inner room, his entire body covered with a blanket, pleading in a deep voice that his body if exposed to light would, according to the best physicians, disintegrate. What Mr Sufi was unaware of were the curses he levelled at him after he had left.

'You know you have to pay,' Mr Sufi said.

'Yes, but what I don't know is that I have to pay more.'

Mr Sufi quailed. He looked at the other tenants and was met by menacing scowls. They pressed closer to him and he felt suffocated.

'You can leave if you don't want to pay.'

His words struck at the instinct for shelter in the hearts of his tenants. Several voices assaulted his ears.

'You are a greedy pig!'

'You will die and leave all your money!'

'Bloodthirsty landlord!'

And before he could make his escape he found his face slapped by Mr Rahim. He was stunned. The crowd was stunned as well and fell back, for Mr Sufi was no ordinary man. This gave him the opportunity to withdraw.

The incident disturbed him for many days. Never had tenants been so outrageously rude to him. And he felt especially bitter against Mr Rahim. Many times he had made no demand on Rahim when he failed to pay his rent on the due date. Occasionally he had even condescended to have tea in his poorly-furnished flat. Humiliated now, he could not even have the man prosecuted: the rehearsal of the incident in court would trigger bad publicity for him. He could easily have Mr Rahim assassinated by Gool, but that would knot him permanently to Gool. He raged and brooded, and eventually his anguish precipitated the idea of killing Gool. For was he not the prime cause of his humiliation? Because of Gool he had increased the rent and because of him received the slap on his face.

He spent several hours seeking a moral justification for his idea. Considered in abstraction, his idea was against all laws, whether those of nature, society or religion. But if the character of the intended victim was taken into account then his idea was ethically sound. Many of the films Mr Sufi had seen ended with the annihilation of villains by heroes who suffered no subsequent conscience-pangs. As for being arrested for murder, surely the police would exonerate him — in fact congratulate him for having saved society from a demon.

Having buttressed himself internally, he then gave his attention to translating his idea into action. Should he hire some desperadoes to waylay Gool and stab him in a quiet street, or should he have him run over by a car? After some thought, the hiring of others seemed to him the action of a coward (even films made this explicit enough) which would diminish him in his own eyes. He had to undertake the act himself if it was to be endowed with any nobility. Should he use a knife or a gun? The knife was associated with the common murderer, the masked thug (cinema screens were full of them). The gun was the best weapon. Besides eliminating the victim swiftly and almost painlessly it was the weapon used by civilised men everywhere in their struggle against criminals.

Where should he kill him? In front of his family at home? This did not appeal to his ethical sense. When he was alone with Gool, say at the Zoo Lake? He dismissed this idea as murder there would be strongly suggestive of malevolent premeditation. The best place would be at his premises in High Road as murder there would be in keeping with the character of the place.

But he was faced with an initial difficulty. He did not have a gun, and a law prevented 'non-whites' from purchasing or possessing one. He could perhaps obtain one by paying some white man ten times the price for parting with the weapon illegally, but this did not appeal to his business sense. He was on the verge of abandoning his idea when the thought leapt to his mind that he could buy a gun from Gool and kill him with it. He chuckled at the thought. Surely this would be consummate revenge for him? Not only would he feel compensated for the pain the man had inflicted upon him, but he would also be the instrument of retributive justice. Filled with elation, he rehearsed the murder-plot in his imagination. He would go to Gool's premises, buy a gun by offering him a large financial bait, shoot him through the head and leave. He would then go to the police and tell them he had killed him in self-defence with his own weapon.

He went in his car to High Road, but passed Gool's premises without stopping. He returned there, but again failed to stop. Tormented by indecision, he drove through streets aimlessly. After an hour he gained sufficient courage. He went back to High Road and parked his car behind the Spider. His intention was now diluted with the thought that there was no harm in visiting Gool and that he need not act should circumstances be unfavourable.

'What a surprise!' Gool said, shaking his hand. 'But you look troubled. Come, sit down.'

Gool took a decanter from a cabinet and poured liquor into two glasses.

'This will cheer you up,' Gool said, handing him a glass.

Mr Sufi, while sipping the liquor, considered whether he should make his request or wait till the next day. But Gool was alone and the liquor was warming: he felt he should not postpone matters.

He asked Gool about his family's health and then got the words out:

'I need a gun.'

'Gun?'

Gool looked at him quizzically and then smiled.

'Please don't tell me you want to kill yourself.'

The reference to suicide alarmed him.

'No, no. I need it for self-protection.'

'Who is threatening you? Tell me and tomorrow we will attend his funeral,' Gool said, pouring more liquor into the glasses.

Mr Sufi could not help smiling. Tomorrow he was going to attend Gool's funeral.

'I must have a gun. Here's a cheque.'

'You know it's expensive and illegal.'

He took out his cheque book and pen. He felt certain that Gool's greed would overcome him. He was prepared to write out any sum Gool wanted for he would not live long enough to take it to the bank.

'It will take a few days to get a gun for you.'

'I need a gun now. My tenants are threatening me,' he blurted out.

'Bastards! Who are they?'

He was forced to relate the incident involving Mr Rahim. When he ended his story he was surprised to see Akbar and several men enter the room. He did not know that Gool had touched an alarm button under the table.

'Akbar, will you visit Mr Rahim in "Liberty Mansions" in May Road and tell him to stop playing with Mr Sufi.'

Akbar and the men left.

'Now, that will settle things. In future leave the business of rent-collecting to me and you will have no further trouble.'

'I must have a gun,' he said in desperation, frightened at Gool's intention to collect the rent. He wrote out a cheque recklessly for a very large sum and handed it to Gool.

Gool looked at the cheque indifferently. Then he went towards a cupboard, took out a gun, and returned with it to Mr Sufi. He withdrew the magazine and showed him the cartridges by spilling them in the palm of his hand, then reloaded the magazine, slotted it, and handed him the gun.

Suddenly fear of using the weapon he held penetrated his consciousness and he was seized by nausea, dizziness, and the paralysing realisation that if he killed Gool his gang would avenge him.

'You are not well,' Gool said. 'I think you should go home and rest.'

Gool took the gun and escorted him to his car. He returned and replaced the gun (which contained blank cartridges) in the cupboard. The cheque was on the table; he folded it and put it in his wallet.

Mr Sufi went home, swallowed several aspirin tablets and crept into bed. When he awoke in the evening his wife told him that Mr Rahim had been waiting for several hours to see him.

Mr Rahim had brought the money. His face was bruised, his eyes swollen and dark.

'I am very sorry . . . The others put me up to it . . . I am grateful to live in your building . . . I have children . . . '

Mr Sufi understood his terror and a feeling of pity burgeoned within him, pity that had never entered his relationship with his tenants — for it had always been a firm tenet of his that a sympathetic landlord would not remain in possession of his properties for long.

He took the money, counted it, then put some back into the envelope and handed it to Mr Rahim.

'You needn't pay the increased amount.'

Mr Rahim, surprised by the magnanimity, left the building a bewildered man.

At the end of the month Gool called Mr Sufi over to High Road.

'To-day is rent-collecting day. Let us go together.'

He had forgotten about Gool's intention to become his rent-collector. He was now filled with dismay, for not only would his tenants see him associating openly with Gool, but the gangster would require a fee for his services.

'Gool, the rent is usually paid to my book-keeper in Mint Road. Only after the seventh of the month does he give me a list of those who have not paid.'

'I see. Then on the eighth I will go with you.'

He left, feeling thankful. If Gool had proposed that in future all rent was to be paid to him at his premises, he would have had to agree. He regretted that he had thought of killing Gool. He had always abhorred violence (apart from the entertaining variety in

45

cinemas) and he wondered what demon had given him the idea.

Gool's intention to be his escort threatened to deprive him of the pleasure of what he considered to be work. He would visit the tenants who had failed to pay; listen patiently to their excuses; assert his authority over them by reminding them of their negligence and irresponsibility; at times complain of the expense of maintaining his properties and the exorbitant rates and taxes he paid; or sternly remind them that failure to pay could have serious legal consequences. The few days a month he spent collecting arrear rents provided his conscience with the anodyne that he worked as everybody else did.

On the eighth of the month the book-keeper sent him the usual list and Gool telephoned to say that he was ready to be his escort.

He was expecting only Gool to accompany him, but when he reached High Road Akbar and Faizel also seated themselves in his car. Exposing himself in public with Gool was bad enough, but to be seen in the company of his companions was certain to bring about a total collapse of his respectability. Moreover, he found sharing the same motor-car with them morally disgusting.

They did not experience much trouble collecting outstanding rent. Most of the tenants had the money ready. A few who did not have the money, seeing their landlord's new associates, apologised profusely and promised to pay before evening. One tenant in 'Fairmont Mansions' who promised to pay before evening was Mrs Hansa whose husband was a commercial traveller. She appeared at the door clad in a flimsy night-dress with her morning-gown flung over her shoulders. She had been combing her hair and attending to her make-up. When she saw the men she gathered her gown closer, exposing the outlines of her lithe body. She was a fair woman, with almond-shaped eyes, a delicately moulded nose and fleshy lips.

'I am sorry about the delay, Mr Sufi. My husband should be arriving from Durban this afternoon. I shall send him over to pay before evening.'

She smiled pleasantly at the men.

'Forgive us for troubling you,' Gool said chivalrously.

'No trouble,' she answered, smiling radiantly at Gool.

'Mr Sufi,' Gool said. 'I think we can rely on her.'

The men took their leave. After collecting the rent from one other tenant, Gool said to Akbar:

'Will you go on with Mr Sufi? I will meet you all later in the car.'

Gool went up a flight of steps and knocked at Mrs Hansa's door. She was now dressed. She was wearing a flounced black skirt and a pale yellow blouse. A string of blue beads encircled her neck. Her black hair cascaded over her shoulders.

'Mr Sufi wants you to make some tea for us, please,' Gool said, surveying her with admiration.

'With pleasure.'

'If you don't mind I will wait for them here.'

She led Gool into the lounge of the flat.

'Sit down. I won't be long with the tea.'

'Wait,' Gool said, holding her by the wrist. 'Surely your husband is not returning today, is he?'

'How do you know?' she said, laughing.

'A guess,' Gool said, flashing a smile and tightening his grip on her wrist.

'Let me get the tea ready.'

'Forget the tea. Come, sit down, and tell me more about the man in Durban.'

Mr Sufi, Akbar and Faizel waited nearly an hour in the car for Gool. When he arrived he was smiling broadly.

'She's a mermaid,' he said, getting in. 'Knows how to wriggle.'

Mr Sufi was puzzled. But when Gool went on to say, 'The one in the gown is a jolly tenant,' he realised whom he referred to and what he meant. He started the car and Gool laughingly advised him:

'You should get rid of that book-keeper agent and do the rent-collecting yourself.'

Faizel made a rude remark and Akbar and Gool laughed loudly. Mr Sufi was riled by their behaviour. In his attitude towards his tenants he had always been morally correct, taking no advantage of the women while the men were at work. Even his own women had been acquired according to custom and religious sanction. Gool's adulterous mating with Mrs Hansa in 'Fairmont Mansions' was a gross, monstrous transgression he could never exonerate. He felt he was in the presence of rotting offal.

'He is a sly one,' Gool said, looking at Mr Sufi. 'Keeps a woman in every mansion.'

'Like sailors who have one in every port,' Akbar said.

They laughed.

'Mr Sufi, you have not introduced us to any of your pets.'

47

'I no longer keep them. Only two are left and they are tenants.'

'You must introduce us to the two that are around.'

The car stopped in front of 'Nirvana Mansions'.

'The next mermaid is yours, Akbar,' Gool said, opening the door of the car.

'She will know how to wriggle,' Akbar answered, in confident expectation of making a catch.

There was only one family in 'Nirvana Mansions' who had not paid rent and Mr Sufi led the way to the flat. It was the same flat in which Olga had lived previously. As he walked along the corridor he felt a poignant sense of loss mingled with yearning.

The knock on the door brought forth Mrs Hafiz, a middle-aged homely sort of woman dressed dowdily. Akbar's face showed disappointment. Mr Sufi asked for the rent. She said her husband was inside and he could speak to him. They entered the lounge. Mr Hafiz was relaxing beside a radio, reading a newspaper. Two small girls were playing with dolls in a corner of the room. Mr Hafiz, without rising from his chair, asked the guests to sit down.

'We haven't much time,' Akbar said curtly, looking offended.

'I have come to collect your rent, Mr Hafiz,' Mr Sufi said.

'I am out of work at the moment, but I have been promised a job next week. I shall pay at the end of the month.'

'Mr Sufi cannot wait,' Akbar said, becoming angry.

'If you don't mind, I am speaking to my landlord.'

'Mr Hafiz . . . '

It was a swift lunging movement by Akbar that left Mr Sufi stunned. Akbar grabbed Mr Hafiz, seemed to lift him out of his arm-chair, and punched him on the face with a crunching blow. Faizel rushed at the man as he fell back into the chair and attacked him. Mrs Hafiz, standing in the doorway, screamed and ran towards her wailing children and cried out, 'Stop! Stop!'

She screamed frantically, clutching the children.

'That's enough,' Gool said, intervening. 'Cheeky swine! Let's go.'

Mr Hafiz lay on the floor, blood flowing from his mouth and nose. Mr Sufi, shocked by the suddenness of the violence, stood in disbelief, fearful, horrified, his mind still a chaos of whirling fists, faces, bodies, blood, and hysterical cries. His legs trembled uncontrollably. He tottered to the bathroom, put his mouth under the tap, drank some water and splashed some over his face.

48

When he rejoined his companions they were going out of the door. Mrs Hafiz and the children were weeping. People had gathered in the corridor, but the four men passed through without looking at them.

'Shocked you a bit,' Gool said to Mr Sufi in the street, placing his arm over his shoulder.

Gool looked unperturbed, as though nothing had happened.

'One must never be soft with tenants,' he added.

Gool had stated the principle which had shaped Mr Sufi's attitude towards his tenants, a principle whose lack of compassion he had now seen exemplified in the raw, aggressive, blind violence of the gangsters. And that the violence should have occurred in the apartment where he had luxuriated in Olga's tropical bed inflated the enormity and horror of it. He had been a strict landlord, exacting every cent owed to him by tenants, at times invoking the aid of the law in evicting them, but he had never dreamt of behaving violently. He had kept his moral perspective clear. The experience in 'Nirvana Mansions' fused into a consciousness already anguished and distended by the bizarre tenor of his life since his involvement with Gool.

'We all need a drink,' Gool said, looking at Mr Sufi.

They adjourned the quest for rent and returned to High Road for refreshments. Later, they continued the quest. But for Mr Sufi the charm of what he had considered to be work was completely subverted so that when Gool began collecting the rents — and put the money into his own pocket saying, 'In future send me the list and leave the rest to me,' — he conceded helplessly.

The disenchantment brought into sharp definition his parallel relationship to the gangsters. He and they lived parasitically off others, spending their lives with playthings — billiards, women, motor-cars — and eternally seeking entertainment in cinemas. He and they had never accomplished a day's work, work that contributed to the sum of man's creative labour. His money-minting properties had been acquired through inheritance; the income of the gangsters was a sort of inheritance received from those who were weak and fearful.

As the quest for rent progressed he was nettled by guilt and constricted by a desire to return to Mr Hafiz, to find out if he had recovered, to apologise, comfort his wife and take the children into his arms. A band of mongols had swooped upon an innocent family and ravaged their domestic peace. He began to fear for the safety of his own family. His small daughters also played with dolls. He yearned to be with them, a feeling that had not come to him when he had spent nights with his concubines. Then the iron gate was protection enough. His imagination lit up with garish realism times when tenants were being evicted and he stood by looking at them indifferently as they were hustled with their belongings out into the street, the children looking bewildered among the furniture and household articles, the shelterless parents standing near him with appealing crestfallen faces.

When Mr Sufi returned home at five o'clock in the afternoon, he felt his ordeal had ended. But with the approach of evening Gool came to fetch him.

'We are having a party to work off today's nasty business. Come, there will be lovely women.'

He accompanied Gool, a prisoner. As they descended the stairs Gool said:

'It is a pleasure to go down lit stairs.'

'Yes,' he answered, looking at the burning lamps. He skipped a step and stumbled. Gool, with a swift action of his hand, held him.

'Even lit stairs can be dangerous,' Gool advised.

As Mr Sufi stepped into the foyer, passed through the doorway, crossed the pavement and seated himself in the Spider, Gool's admonitory words echoed abrasively within him; they seemed to hold some oracular meaning. But the thought-annihilating thunder of the starting car, the recoil of his body as the car hurtled through the street, the swift succession of shop-front pillars, denied him any possibility of the grace of insight.

On the way to High Road Gool said:

'The more women at the party, the merrier it will be. Let's get some of yours.'

'They are tenants,' he protested feebly.

'All the better. Let's round them up.'

Mr Sufi directed Gool to a building. When the car stopped, he said he would fetch a former mistress. He returned with Sadia after pleading with her that he wished to take her to a party and had no other intention. When she had objected that she didn't want to be 'tricked or used', he had reminded her of his honesty.

As Sadia came up to the car, she hesitated. Gool quickly emerged from the car, addressed her gallantly and, opening the door of the Spider, had her seated before she could change her mind.

At the next building Mr Sufi had no trouble. Marina, much to his consternation, said:

'Anytime is party time. After all I am free.'

Her sardonic words were spawned by the remembered bitterness of a broken relationship. They evoked within him a time when she was bound to him and he was free to take pleasure with any of his women.

When they reached High Road, they found men and women in a gay mood. Gool introduced his companions. To Mr Sufi's gratitude, Gool made no mention of his former relationship with Sadia and Marina; he mercifully spared him the embarrassment the revelation would have caused and the curiosity it would have aroused. Gool invited everybody over to the bar which was situated in a corner of the dining-room. Drinks were served. Mr Sufi was glad to observe that Sadia and Marina drank orange juice. Soon supper was ready.

'Sit beside Eve,' Gool said to Mr Sufi as they moved towards the table laden with food for gourmets.

Eve was a tall woman in a shining black dress that concealed her scraggy figure. Her face was plastered with make-up, her dark eyes were adorned with fiercely blackened brows and she wore a three-tiered wig.

'I love landlords,' she said. 'They are so cute.'

She laughed so loudly that Mr Sufi marvelled that a voice so herald-like could issue from her wafer-thin lips.

'Ladies and gentlemen,' Gool addressed the company, 'enjoy yourselves. But before you begin I wish to thank, on everyone's behalf, our patron and friend, Mr Sufi, for his presence.'

Everyone applauded and Eve brushed her partner's cheek with a kiss. Her lips were moist with wine.

Mr Sufi scarcely enjoyed his supper, or rather Eve's supper, for she persisted in taking morsels of food from her plate with her fork and stuffing them into his mouth (much to the amusement of those nearby). When her plate was empty she took his plate and began to feed him with what lay in it, so that by the time supper ended he was feeling thoroughly bloated and uncomfortable. To add to the meal's agony he had tried to keep watch on Sadia and Marina and had been needled by jealousy

51

when he saw them enjoying themselves immensely in the company of Gool and Akbar.

After supper they all went to the lounge for coffee, cigars and party chit-chat. Gool lit a cigar and put it into Mr Sufi's mouth. Then he sat down on a settee and placed his arm around Sadia, and Mr Sufi, sitting opposite him, found his lap to be the seat of the mirthful Eve who, besides obstructing his view of his former concubines, wriggled annoyingly in his lap and presented him with the problem of keeping his cigar away from her dress.

Later dancing began. Mr Sufi had never danced in his life. Despite his protests Eve took him on the floor. He shuffled awkwardly, tramped on her shoes, stumbled. Eve held him, her face a smirking mask. Gool dancing with Sadia and Akbar with Marina floated gracefully past him, the gentle light from the lamps playing on their faces.

Eve took Mr Sufi to the bar. 'You need another drink to loosen up,' she said. Gool and Sadia arrived after them. Gool ordered wine for Sadia. Mr Sufi watched unbelievingly as Sadia took the glass of wine and put it to her lips. She had been one of his favourites, plump, petite, learned in religious mottoes. Now she drank wine like an infidel.

When they rejoined the dancers, Mr Sufi was appalled to find that a saturnalian atmosphere was beginning to prevail. Several women had removed some upper clothing, displaying bare backs and shoulders. What he had seen on cinema screens was a reality before him. The music swelled into a tempest and he found himself, as Eve drew him among the frenzied dancers, overcome by a madness, a fermentation within. The swift pulse of the music penetrated him, and he jigged and jived and capered and shook, urged on by the demented, serpent-like Eve.

During pauses in the dancing Eve took Mr Sufi to the bar for more drinks. When he could no longer hold a glass with steady fingers, she led him to a bedroom. His mind swollen with discordant images and his ears throbbing with wild music, he was unable to satisfy her. She left him, cursing, to seek another partner. Overcome by fatigue and stupor, he fell asleep.

He awoke when several hands lifted him and deposited him on the floor. He heard voices and opening his eyes saw in the livid light that entered through an open window Gool's form above that of Sadia on the bed. Nausea and horror seized him. They seemed to be enacting a brutalised, gross parody of his former erotic life. A painful pressure began to constrict his head; he tried to lift himself; he seemed to be fighting against a macabre darkness. Then, abruptly, his consciousness blew out.

He awoke to the sound of a piercing voice, a voice within him, though its source seemed external. He touched his face, his body, the floor, trying to establish his existence in a particular time and place in the presence of two slumbering bodies entangled on a bed a few feet away from him.

With effort he rose and moved towards the door. He found himself in a larger room. In the pale light that pervaded it he saw bodies lying on the floor and on several couches. The room's distorted perspective revealed to him a distant purple door. He stepped warily past entwined bodies. Inadvertently stepping on an outstretched hand that shrieked 'Swine!' he found himself catapulted head foremost against a wall. He reached the door, and opening it found himself in a room where an assembly of august personages were seated around a formidable table on which sprouted a brilliant green pasture. A white bull grazed among a herd of red and black cattle. The personages looked at him with contempt as he passed through to another door that gave access into a dark tunnel. Touching the walls on either side of him he journeyed through until he was confronted by the last door. He felt the lock and turned the handle.

The street lamps were burning in the grey light of morning. He stood for a while on the pavement and looked at the houses as though he had strayed into a foreign suburb. When he saw the Spider in the street he awoke to full consciousness. He scanned the street to see if there was anyone about who would recognise him. Then he hurried homewards.

Ten

Brooding over his broken life, the thought of killing Gool came to Mr Sufi again. As long as Gool existed he would be his quarry. He had failed to kill him in the way he had planned, but his failure had been due to his folly in trying to undertake the act himself. In fact, what he had done was to confirm Gool's power over him. Now, more urgently than before, the man had to be killed. But how? And by whom? After many days and nights the idea came to him like a sudden revelation. He was the patron of the supermen of the Spartan Gymnasium. The supermen were hunks of muscle without intelligence. All he had to do was to order them into action against Gool and the result would be predictable. Gool would either be killed or given such a fright that he would never trouble him again. The whole operation seemed so simple that he decided to telephone Riad immediately. He dialled four digits, then his finger froze as indecision gripped him. Riad's members were supermen, but they were men nevertheless. He had to convince them by rational argument that what he wanted them to do was morally and socially right. They would listen to him and since they would be sensible of how he could reward them, they would carry out his wish.

He spent many hours spinning the argument he would use to spur the supermen into action. When he felt satisfied, he telephoned Riad.

'Listen Riad, can I meet you this evening together with the three men who took part in the contest at the Avalon? I have something to tell you.'

'Of course, Mr Sufi. We will do anything for you.'

He met them at the door of the restaurant. They were nattily dressed, their clothes fitting their powerful bodies perfectly. They shook Mr Sufi's hand and Brutus applied his usual vice-grip. Mr Sufi accepted it stoically.

A receptionist ushered them into a pine-wood cubicle with a beaded curtain and a trellis with intertwining leaves overhead. They sat down on chairs around a candle-lit table.

While sipping fruit drinks Mr Sufi asked Riad if the gymnasium was progressing.

'Your cheque did wonders. You should come and have a look.'

'And exercise as well,' Brutus said, lifting his hand above his head as though he were holding up a dumb-bell. He laughed in a gay baritone voice.

'Of course,' Mr Sufi agreed. 'A patron must not remain in the background.'

The first course of the meal was served: cream-of-mushroom soup flavoured with mint and spice.

'How many hours do you all spend in the gymnasium every day?'

'Three to four,' Riad replied. 'It's hard training, but it has its rewards.'

'Rewards?'

'Health, strength and beauty.'

'Of course health and beauty are true rewards. But strength? Of what use is strength that isn't used, like armour in the museum?'

'We are not after strength,' Julius said. 'It sort of comes by the way.'

'Perhaps you exercise to win contests?'

'Only I do,' Brutus said, looking at his companions. Everyone laughed.

The second course was served: grilled peri-peri prawns and lobsters garnished with salad, olives and lemons.

'For how many months must one exercise before one can win a contest?'

'Months!' Brutus cried in a muted voice.

'I have been training for ten years,' Julius answered.

'Ten years!'

'Yes, and I haven't won a trophy yet. Brutus always snatches it from me.'

There was merriment.

'Perfection takes time,' Riad said.

'It is perhaps a lot of wasted effort to win a trophy. You should be given countries to govern.'

'We also exercise to win women,' Brutus said, with an arch glint in his eyes.

Everyone laughed.

'You must have a harem,' Mr Sufi said.

Riad smiled.

'I disagree about exercise bringing us women. Mr Sufi is a great Romeo and we don't stand a chance against him.'

Mr Sufi enjoyed the compliment.

'Actually the gymnasium and women don't go together,' Riad continued. 'I advise my members to keep away from women.'

They ate in silence for a while. Mr Sufi was quite content with the drift of the conversation. He had already presented in embryo the substance of his argument and would have no difficulty in going on to elaborate it and make the proposal he had in mind.

'I agree with you, Riad, about women,' Mr Sufi said. 'They weaken you so that you can't face up to life's problems.'

'That's the advantage of being in a gymnasium. You forget the world and its problems,' Anthony said.

'A little selfish, isn't it? I mean trying to run away from life?'

'No, no,' Brutus interjected. 'We don't run away from life. We strengthen our bodies to face life.'

'That's a sensible statement. Let's examine it a little. There is your strength which you gain by exercising your bodies for many years. But to what end? Can you give an example of how you will use it?'

'Strength can be useful when you are attacked,' Julius answered.

'Excellent! In this world criminals are all around us and we have to protect ourselves.'

The next course on the menu was served: spiced roast chicken, fillet steak, rice, herb-flavoured sauce and a variety of condiments.

Before they started eating, Mr Sufi took out an envelope from his pocket and handed it to Riad who looked a little puzzled.

'Open it. It is a donation.'

Riad smiled, opened the envelope and found a cheque. He looked at the cheque with satisfaction and handed it to Brutus who blinked his eyes several times and smilingly gave it to Julius.

Julius stared at the cheque in disbelief and handed it to Anthony who examined it, whistled, and returned it to Riad.

'Thank you, Mr Sufi,' Riad said gratefully.

'To go back to our discussion about strength,' Mr Sufi went on. 'What good is your strength to you if you are not attacked? In fact, because of your strength you will not be attacked. This brings us back to the question of its use.'

'Mr Sufi,' said Riad, 'you must not talk in this way. You will discourage my members and close the gymnasium down.'

Everyone burst into laughter and Brutus slapped Mr Sufi's back. Fortunately, his arms were resting against the table and he was able to withstand the blow. The conversation now veered to films and Mr Sufi did not pursue his argument. He wanted them to enjoy the food and feel relaxed.

But when dessert arrived — fruit salad, pistachio ice-cream covered with a mantle of chocolate and crowned with cherries — he raised the question of strength again.

'I believe that if strength is not used positively, for instance against criminals, and is allowed to lie dead in you, it is a defect. Strength is not something like an ornament. What is your opinion, Brutus?'

The argument threatened the single-minded devotion of the Herculean quartet to physical perfection. They had spent so many years of their lives in the gymnasium that they felt they were useless men, like the antiquated armour Mr Sufi had spoken of.

'I agree,' Brutus replied. 'But can we take on what the police are supposed to do?'

'No, but there are some people who go on doing wrong without anyone stopping them.'

Mr Sufi kept silent for a while to allow them to realise that he wished to enlist their aid.

The final item on the menu arrived: coffee and pastries.

'Friends,' said Mr Sufi, 'let me tell you what I have in mind. I am sure you will agree with me that while health and beauty are good in themselves, strength must be put to use. I don't say we should set out to destroy criminals, but we should put fear into them at least. For instance, we have the gangster Gool who goes about threatening people. Surely we can prevent him?'

For a moment the four men stopped drinking coffee and eating pastries as though they had suddenly discovered that Gool was eavesdropping. They sat like wax-work figures, eternally doomed to remain seated around a candle-lit table. Riad was the first to recover. As a tenant he knew that Mr Sufi had never shown a social conscience.

'We will have to think over the matter.'

'I am prepared to go on supporting your gymnasium . . . pay all the expenses . . . give you each a cheque.'

'We exercise for fun only . . . really.'

Brutus, Julius and Anthony looked stupidly into their cups.

'The other thing,' Riad continued in a conciliatory voice, 'is that we are something like Yogis, only we attend to our bodies rather than our souls. We don't care much about the world.'

'You had some lovely women on the stage,' Mr Sufi reminded him.

'They were only there to attract spectators.'

'I see,' Mr Sufi said, smiling ironically, desperately trying to conceal his disappointment. 'Anyway, consider my offer. I am only trying to do something for society.'

'We will think about it,' Riad concluded, rising from his chair. 'We must go now.'

Brutus offered Mr Sufi a limp hand.

Eleven

One went up a flight of tiled stairs in a handsomely designed modern building in Mint Road to reach the office of the Editor of *Glitter*. In case one strayed there were six tablets gleaming with silver arrows and the inscription 'Editor-in-Chief: *Glitter*' to guide the visitor to his office. One came to a door topped by a framed oblong glass on which the following words blazed in luminous orange: '*Glitter* — The Paper by the Indians, for the Indians, and of the Indians. Be proud of it!' Inside the office, which was expensively furnished, carpeted and wall-papered, with venetian blinds covering two large windows, was the Editor. Faizel Adil was busily tapping on his typewriter. He was a lean, curly-haired, doe-eyed man dressed in tight-fitting gaudy clothing. He was below average height with the manner of a restless schoolboy. He tapped on his typewriter, referred to various note-books scattered on the table, looked at some papers in a tray, asked his secretary — a prim, mini-skirted girl with an Afro-wig sitting at the table near him — to sharpen a pencil; and then, as though some urgent matter had suddenly arisen, phoned several people. His secretary hardly did any work; she sat in her plush chair, did some knitting, read magazines, made tea, and displayed her ebony legs to the visitor.

'*Glitter* is the only paper exclusively for Indians and the kick-off has been just great,' the Editor said to the visitor from behind his glass-topped executive-type oak desk. 'Sales are sky-rocketing. Fifty thousand copies have been sold within a few days and what would anybody expect after all the brainstorming I do. I work twenty hours out of the twenty-four. I am a human dynamo. If you know of anyone interested in journalism, send him to me. I require top-grade reporters, men with guts. You know what I mean.'

He jumped out of his chair, went out of his office to the balcony, exercised with a couple of dumb-bells, took a few deep breaths, posed like a body-builder, and returned. 'I have to keep fit in the newspaper game,' he said, jumping into his revolving chair and spinning around.

The first issue of *Glitter* was priced at five cents. The entire first page was devoted to a policy statement by the Editor-in-Chief: '*Glitter* is going to be a great weekly chronicle, a pool in which the community will see itself, a community at play, at work, at social functions. But we are definitely not going to pull our punches when it comes to bashing the community when it needs bashing. We mean business, serious business. We are not interested in who gets hurt in the process. But if there is one thing we are not going to get ourselves messed· up in it is politics. *Glitter* will not play the politicians' dirty game, whether White or Black . . . '

The first issue of *Glitter* antagonised all those interested in politics. And Dr Kamal, president of the Orient Front, issued a statement that *Glitter* was a 'racist newspaper financed by Whites to undermine and divide the Blacks.'

The first issue also antagonised all Hindus. An article by Aziz Khan on 'Islam and Polygamous Marriages' included the following paragraph: 'The lust of Hindus for the wives of others is amply demonstrated by the sculpture in the Ajanta caves in India. What could be more odious to the Muslim male glorying in the felicity offered by his several wives in the sanctuary of his home than the sight of the promiscuous contortions of the human animal in coition as represented in the caves? Surely the art of a civilisation is a product of its morality. Islamic art is unrivalled for its purity.'

The second issue of *Glitter* failed to appear on time. It appeared after a month due, the Editor-in-Chief declared, 'to various difficulties best known to knowledgeable tycoons in the press game.' The price of the paper was now twenty cents. The headlines proclaimed: 'African Dolls Invade Fordsburg'. A sub-heading stated: 'Forty Indians lured away by black sirens every night'.

The article gave an account of 'large-busted African call girls from Soweto driving posh American limousines' invading Fordsburg every night 'to carry away Indian males like helpless victims.' In an interview a certain Ismail Yusuf gave a detailed account of his experiences with the Soweto sirens, concluding: 'No normal man can satisfy their super-hot demands.'

The second issue also contained two pages of letters from readers. One correspondent stated that the 'dynamic Editor-in-Chief has hit the Indian world with a big load of TNT;' another from India said that 'Glitter is unique in newspaper printing history as it caters exclusively for Indians outside India;' another that 'the Editor-in-Chief has descended on the Asian scene like a fiery comet.'

A number of male readers of the second issue, aspirant victims of the dolls, walked the suburban streets several nights in succession, but to no avail.

It seemed that the third issue of Glitter would never appear, though the presence of the Editor typing feverishly in his office and exercising on the balcony suggested that it would eventually be printed. It appeared after an interval of three months. There was no explanation for the delay this time. The price was now fifteen cents. The main story appeared under the headline: 'School Scandal Rocks Community'.

'Four Fordsburg schoolgirls have claimed that they have been forced to leave school by their headmaster because they were eight months pregnant. They refused to reveal the names of the males involved, but hinted that several teachers and senior pupils were responsible. An inquiry spearheaded by Glitter and its newspaper sleuths soon made incriminating finds – contraceptives were found in several classrooms. Glitter is now able to reveal that our schools are hot-beds of corruption and vice, dens of drug-taking and marijuana-smoking where sexy schoolgirls sprint from desk to desk. It is to the credit of Glitter and its staff that the vice going on in our educational institutions has now been made public.' The story ended with a comment by 'the renowned Islamic scholar Aziz Khan' who said that the Muslim community was 'facing a moral storm and crisis.'

Faizel Adil walked up the stairs to his office listlessly. He sat down in his chair and looked at the chair near him, his former secretary's. She had left because for the past three months he had not been able to pay her her salary. On his left were stacks of unsold previous issues of *Glitter* which he had collected from various shops and cafés after the delivery of the third issue. In a tray on the table were bills from the printer, the funiture dealer, the motor-car dealer and others. There was also a reminder from the landlord of unpaid rent. He rolled up the bills into cylinders and put them back in the tray.

Why had his paper failed to sell? Had he erred, he reflected, by believing the public to be essentially naive, foolish and gossip-hungry, requiring to be fed on a diet of melodramatic reports? He looked at the bills again and a pith of bitterness against the public hardened within him. He clenched his fists involuntarily.

He became aware of a buzzing sound. At first he thought it was from somewhere in the building, but as the sound increased in intensity he realised it was from the street. He went outside on the balcony and saw droves of school children assembling below him. They were carrying accusatory placards: '*Glitter* is Yellow'; '*Glitter* = Dirt'; 'Down with the Editor-in-Chief!' They began screaming and jeering at him.

He reacted by smiling and waving at the demonstrating pupils. Then he quickly went to his office, returned with his camera, and began taking photographs. He shouted at the pupils to show 'more guts' in their demonstration. It occurred to him that he was in an ideal position to deliver an oration.

'Silence! Silence!' he shouted.

The pupils, conditioned to taking orders, quietened.

'For the first time in history a newspaper appears for the exclusive benefit of the Indian community, and what does the community do? Bloody nothing! There are stacks of unsold papers in shops and cafés. Do you think that by not buying the paper you will make me close shop? My livelihood does not depend on your miserable cents. Do you understand? You duped fools!'

The pupils began howling. A fire was lit on the pavement with copies of *Glitter*. Faizel Adil shouted, 'That's great!' He would not let them triumph; the final victory would be his. He ran into his office and returned with a bundle of copies of *Glitter* and threw it down into the blaze. He brought more bundles and threw them down.

'Burn them! Burn them!' he shouted and laughed hysterically.

Twelve

Faizel Adil came to interview Mr Sufi. When he had telephoned him and said that he wished to speak to him in order to verify certain allegations made by his tenants, Mr Sufi had refused to see him; but when Adil explained that he would only have himself to blame if the public received a prejudiced report given by his tenants, he reluctantly consented.

Fawzia opened the gate to him.

'I am the Editor of *Glitter*. I have an appointment with Mr Sufi.'

She led him into the reception room next to her father's office. A variety of indoor plants — lovingly tended by Fawzia — gave an atmosphere of tranquillity to the room. She entered the office and announced the Editor's arrival.

'Tell him to come in.'

Mr Sufi was seated at his desk, examining some fresh bills that had been sent by shops having business dealings with Gool, among them one from Tabriz Gallery, a Persian carpet emporium.

'I am Faizel Adil, the editor of *Glitter*.'

He shook Mr Sufi's hand and sitting down on a chair took a notebook out of his bag, as well as past issues of *Glitter* which he handed to Mr Sufi.

'I have come to interview you, firstly, to authenticate — I am sure you understand the meaning of the word — a report that you are employing outlaws to threaten and beat up tenants. You had a tenant who complained about increased rent, and another who could not pay his rent because he was out of work, assaulted and terrorised by outlaws. What have you to say? Remember, as a journalist, I do not fear any man.'

'That's good,' Mr Sufi said, reflectively. 'Tell me, Mr Adil, what is your age?'

'Twenty-eight and an Editor.'

'Twenty-eight and very clever.'

'My profession demands a great deal of knowledge, Mr Sufi.'

'If you don't mind, I should like to give you some advice. Why don't you write about things that interest the public, things like rape, suicide, love-affairs, elopements, and leave the property business to those who know about such things.'

'My newspaper has a social concern . . . '

'There is nothing social about property. It is strictly a business. For instance , here on my desk are some bills sent to me by people I have no dealings with. I have to settle the matter myself. I don't have to go to a newspaper editor to complain that someone is trying to cheat me.'

'If I were to listen to you no one would buy my paper. Now, to get back. Besides the allegations I have mentioned I have received another report. It refers to complaints by tenants about your properties. I intend publishing both reports if you don't have anything to say.'

'Well, what are the complaints about my properties?'

'Your tenants speak of unpainted walls, blocked drains, toilets that don't flush properly, ceilings that are collapsing, dangerous balconies, corridors and stairs that are unlit . . . '

'Mr Adil!'

Mr Sufi rose from his seat, his face flushing as a turbid disorder swirled within him. Impulsively he picked up a letter-opening stiletto that lay on his desk.

'Leave my office now . . . '

Adil jumped up with his notebook and bag in hand, retreated to the door, closed it and left hurriedly.

He ran to the gate and found it locked. Fawzia, who was reading a magazine while reclining in a patio chair on the balcony, saw Adil looking flustered.

'What's the matter?' she asked, going up to him.

'No, nothing. Open the gate please.'

She opened the gate and he passed through. He paused on the stair-landing after the gate was safely locked, looked at Fawzia and said:

'You are beautiful!' Then he bounded down the stairs.

Mr Sufi sat down in his chair to calm himself. He began to realise that he had erred in losing self-control. If Adil published the information he had, he would damage whatever respect the public still had for him. He would give Adil enough time to return to his office, then telephone him to come back and complete the interview.

He looked at the copies of *Glitter* Adil had left on the table. He had seen the paper before but had never bought one. He turned the pages and read various paragraphs. A tremor of fear shot through him. If Adil did not come back, he must go to him and tell him his side of the story. Tenants were not entirely innocent and their grievances failed to reflect their own shortcomings, which were many. They were given to vandalism and wastage; they did not appreciate his own expenses in taxes and maintenance charges; their children were little better than hooligans; they were dirty in their personal habits; they failed to pay rent when due; and many were under the impression that his apartment buildings belonged to a charity organisation. He would tell Adil the truth of what happened on the two occasions when the 'outlaws' were involved; in fact he would confess to Adil how Gool was blackmailing him. Adil would pity him and perhaps even come to his rescue by exposing in his newspaper the activities of the 'outlaws'.

He feverishly looked up Adil's telephone number in a copy of *Glitter* and dialled.

'I am sorry, Mr Adil, for losing control of myself. Please forgive me. Can you come over to complete the interview?'

'You are not my landlord!' Adil shouted, replacing the telephone on its cradle.

Mr Sufi held the telephone in his hand for a while, shaken by the tart rebuff. He telephoned again and told Adil that if he published anything that was defamatory he would engage an army of lawyers to sue him.

'Did you say lawyers?' Adil asked, bursting into cynical laughter.

Riled, Mr Sufi telephoned Gool but stopped after dialling four numbers. The thought occurred to him that if Gool threatened or punished Adil he would have first-hand evidence of his complicity with the 'outlaws'. His threat of prosecution was sufficiently potent to deter him from publishing anything damaging.

The fourth issue of *Glitter* appeared so long after Adil had interviewed Mr Sufi that he had forgotten the existence of the man. He bought a copy at a street corner and recoiled at what he saw — it seemed as if a black gargoyle disgorged a torrent of fetid vomit on him: 'Greedy Landlord Threatens Tenants With Outlaws'. A smaller gargoyle croaked: 'Building collapses on tenants'.

The article began: 'A well-known landlord is resorting to gangland tactics to terrorise tenants who complain . . .'

He angrily folded the paper, rushed home, then re-opened it and read the entire article. Though no mention was made of his name, it would be obvious to many people that he was the landlord involved. And the word 'outlaws' gored him: it linked him with conspirators, anarchists and rebels. Adil had to be crushed, bullets pumped into his sciolist's cranium.

He telephoned Gool who told him to come over to High Road with the newspaper.

Gool read the report.

'What will you do to him, Gool?'

'He needs a visit. Come.'

They found Adil exercising with dumb-bells on the balcony.

'In the newspaper game one must keep fit,' he said as they came up to him. He held the dumb-bells above his head with difficulty.

'We are not here to watch you exercise,' Gool said in a menacing tone. Gool took the dumb-bells from Adil's hands and placed them on the floor.

Adil, trying to look brave, led the visitors into his office and asked them to sit down.

'Now, gentlemen, do you wish to make a statement to the press?'

'Who wrote this report about the "outlaws"?' Gool asked, throwing the paper on the table.

'One of my journalists. But it does not refer to you or to Mr Sufi . . . There are other landlords and other . . .'

'Other what?'

'It does not refer to you, Gool.'

'Adil,' Mr Sufi said, 'didn't you come to see me over some complaints by tenants?'

'You are mistaken. I have never come to you.'

'Liar!'

Mr Sufi, infuriated, rose from his chair, and shook both his fists at Adil. Gool stood up and placed a restraining hand on

Mr Sufi's shoulder. He then addressed Adil.

'Listen, get this clear. I am not going to fire a bullet into you when I can blot you out more cheaply. Go immediately and remove all the copies of your paper from circulation.'

'Yes . . . I will go now.'

'Good.'

As they were going out of the door Gool turned and said to Adil:

'Stick to politics and sport if you want to stay out of trouble.'

In the street Mr Sufi told Gool of the day Faizel Adil came to interview him. At that time he had believed that his threat of court action would have been a sufficient deterrent to prevent Adil from publishing the report.

At High Road, over liquor, Gool said:

'He could have destroyed you.'

'Yes,' Mr Sufi agreed, looking thankfully at his 'protector'.

'You know there is the small matter of the usual fees. I haven't had time to visit you.'

Mr Sufi handed Gool his cheque book.

Gool wrote out a cheque, adding two extra zeros. Mr Sufi signed obligingly.

Thirteen

For Faizel Adil, the visit of Gool and Mr Sufi was not only financially disastrous (he had been forced to withdraw from circulation the entire fourth edition of *Glitter*); it had severely injured his vanity. He thought of revenge, and having enough time in his office to indulge in romantic fantasy, saw himself the hero in the following epic: trapped on a balcony was a princess, guarded by a dragon with stiletto-sharp claws. He was a princely warrior, and though lacking steed, armour and sword, with the pen and the word at his command. He would reach the captive princess and abduct her from her guardian monster.

He began a letter to Fawzia with the prologue: ' "You are beautiful!" These were my immortal words to you when I left you caged on the balcony, O Persian princess, as beautiful as a rose from the gardens of the Taj Mahal . . . '

When he had completed the letter and signed his name he went to 'Orient Mansions'. He felt certain that Fawzia would appear at the gate. He would give her the letter and it would go to work for him.

He climbed the stairs and when he reached the top cautiously looked to see if the princess was standing on the balcony, lost in pensive reverie. There was no one. He pressed the bell-button. He saw Fawzia's form emerging from a doorway and he withdrew a step.

When Fawzia reached the gate she saw no one.

'Fawzia, it's me,' she heard him whisper.

She was slightly shocked, but when she saw Adil crouching to

68

one side and pleadingly offering a letter to her, she recovered.

'Take this letter. Quick!'

He handed her the letter. She hesitated. No one had ever come in this furtive fashion to the gate. The letter fell at her feet.

Adil quickly disappeared down the stairs.

Curious, Fawzia picked up the letter. She returned into the house and her mother asked:

'Who was at the gate, Fawzia?'

'Only a hawker, mother. I sent him away.'

Later, she read the letter several times. Slowly her body chemistry began to respond to the flattering references to her beauty and person and to the call of the male: 'Break open the gate, descend the stairs and come into my arms, your dying-in-love prince . . . '

Fawzia had never received a love letter from anyone. Her ideas of love and marriage were conventional. One day her parents would receive a proposal of marriage from a relative, they would accept, and she would marry the man and love him. Her mother had already been preparing her for her eventual role as wife, and initiating her, with extreme delicacy, into the mysteries of bodily union and child-bearing. Now Adil's letter came to disturb her, with its appeal to her individuality and the power of her being over him. She found herself caught in the subtle joy of being desired and yearned to experience the romantic love he offered her at a secret meeting.

On the pretext that she wanted something from the shops, Fawzia hurried to meet her lover.

It was a brief meeting in a park. She returned home with her ears ringing with Adil's love-rhetoric.

The next meeting led to a succession of others, and after two months Fawzia knew that she was pregnant. She confessed to Adil.

'I must marry you as soon as possible. Tell your father.'

'My father!'

'Tell your mother to tell him if you are afraid. He will come to offer you to me.'

Fawzia, dreading the consequences, confessed to her mother. Her mother was shocked and angry, but after several hours her protective feelings ruled and she began to accept the irreversibility of her daughter's condition. Fawzia must marry Adil as soon as possible. Although there would be gossip, it would come to an end when the couple settled down to domestic life. She would speak to her husband as soon as she found him in an untroubled mood. She had through the days and months sensed the stresses within him, stresses which she knew originated in his nexus with Gool. But her subject position had prevented her from reaching out to him.

She told her husband one night while serving him tea and cake in the dining-room. He had arrived from the cinema where he had seen a comedy.

'Fawzia is pregnant,' she declared firmly.

She felt that a resolutely stated truth would be best as decisive action was needed if Fawzia — and the family — was to be saved from ignominy and disgrace.

'Pregnant?' he enquired vaguely while slicing a cream cake. His wife looked at him, bewildered. Had he failed to hear her? She repeated her words.

He ate some cake and drank some tea. Then he enquired, again vaguely:

'She's not married yet, is she?'

'No,' she said. 'But she must marry Faizel Adil soon.'

She left hurriedly, went to her bedroom and wept.

The revelation had come to him like an instant inner explosion, a silent demolition which left his physical self intact and his neural reflexes functioning normally.

After he had had enough tea and cake, he sat for over an hour in a state of inertia. It was past midnight when his body, tenanted by some mobile being, led him to his bedroom.

Next morning Mr Sufi questioned his wife further and realised that there was nothing else to be done but visit Adil and arrange for his daughter's marriage.

He found Adil playing with a tennis ball on the balcony, flinging it against the wall and catching it skilfully as it rebounded. Mr Sufi stopped a short distance away, fearing to approach nearer as Adil seemed to be working himself into a frenzy, ball and man intertwined in some fierce battle. Suddenly the ball shot back from the wall at a tangent and struck Mr Sufi's head. 'Ha!' Adil shouted, and with incredible acrobatic dexterity leapt at the ball as it rebounded. He caught it with a cry of 'Good catch!' and flung it at Mr Sufi who thrust his hands at the missile. The ball struck his arm and was deflected over the balustrade to the street below. Adil jumped on the balustrade, and waving his arms, shouted at passers-by to retrieve the ball which had rolled under a motor-car. Mr Sufi, fearing that he would fall headlong, rushed towards him to save him.

'Come father,' Adil said, jumping down. 'I can see you have come to offer me something. Where is our friend today?'

They entered the office. Mr Sufi sat down on a chair and pretended not to have heard the question.

'Adil, you will have to marry Fawzia.'

'Any minute, father. Bring the priest. She is beautiful and she is pregnant.'

'Your parents . . . '

'I am an independent man, as you know, with my own newspaper. Nobody controls Faizel Adil's actions.'

Mr Sufi was filled with intense loathing for the man. Man? He seemed to be the spawn of some foul brute and nasty sprite — a little while ago he had been perched on the balustrade, flapping his arms. If he had not come for his daughter's sake, he would have fled.

'You know there are our customs.'

'Of course. I have already told my parents. They will visit you in a day or two. They must hurry, otherwise there is going to be disgrace, for me, for you, Fawzia, the child, everyone.'

'Yes,' Mr Sufi said, a little pleased that Adil was perceptive of the consequences.

'And I shall also soon be in disgrace, father. And all because of your friend. Look at the papers in that tray before you.'

He unrolled the paper cylinders and saw that they were letters of demand from the printer, stationer, furnisher, the landlord, the motor-car dealer and others.

'I may be in jail before the wedding takes place.'

Mr Sufi examined the bills and felt a strange sense of pity for Adil pulse through him as though he too were the victim of an unscrupulous blackmailer. He took out his cheque book and began writing out cheques in payment of the accounts.

'I am grateful,' Adil murmured as a cunning smile crossed his lips.

'You have an expensive car,' Mr Sufi said, writing out the last cheque.

'It helps my image as Editor-in-Chief.' .

The words chilled Mr Sufi; they evoked reverberations of similar words he had heard before.

'Thank you,' Adil said, taking all the cheques from Mr Sufi's hand. 'I will rush my parents with the wedding arrangements.'

'Let them come soon,' Mr Sufi said, rising from his chair. He hoped that his gesture in paying Adil's debts would bind his future son-in-law to him. Though he disliked him intensely, there was the possibility that he might change.

'Your friend ruined me,' Adil said, feigning misery. 'Fawzia will have no wedding-jewellery.'

Mr Sufi looked at him for a moment, then wrote out another cheque.

After Mr Sufi had left, Faizel Adil flung all the cheques in the air and gleefully watched them fall on the table. He chuckled, then laughed uproariously.

Adil's parents failed to arrive, and when after a week Mr Sufi telephoned him he received no answer. He went to Adil's office and found the door locked. He made inquiries from people in the building, but no one knew of Adil's whereabouts or of his family's. As day succeeded day he realised that the man had fled. He told his wife of his suspicion and left it to her to tell Fawzia.

Fawzia was disconsolate for many days. She telephoned Adil's office many times and heard his telephone ring in continuous bursts of mocking metal laughter. She disbelieved her father's story of the cheques he had given Adil until he went to the bank and brought the paid cheques. Her sudden abandonment by her mercurial lover, her yearning for him, her ignominious pregnancy came as a traumatic experience.

Fawzia's agony and fate — who would marry her with an illegitimate child? Or even if the child were given away for adoption? — wrung the fibres of her father's being as nothing else had ever done, not even his involvement with Gool. Earlier the object of his preoccupation and worry had been himself. He now found the dimension of his suffering lifted to a new height. The sight of his daughter, doomed to an unhappy life by that mentally grotesque, sensual monster Faizel Adil (a monster who painfully revealed to him something of his own sensual image) filled him with profound love which he was unable to express, for he had never found the time to become part of the lives of his children. And he was seized by fear for the safety of his other daughters: they too were vulnerable. Love and compassion for them filled him.

To save Fawzia from having an illegitimate child and prevent the inevitable public stigma, he decided to send her to Cape Town to his wife's brother and ask him to arrange an illegal abortion. When he informed his wife of his plan she felt unhappy as she feared for Fawzia's subsequent health, but she bent to her husband's wish. He telephoned his brother-in-law and Fawzia was taken to the airport and sent off.

She returned after a month, looking pale and thin, physically and emotionally drained of life. She felt numb with bewilderment at the disastrous end to her love-affair. Her mother consoled her as best she could — though in private she grieved at her daughter's fate — and undertook the task of restoring her to health again.

Fourteen

With the passage of days the idea that he was being persecuted by supernatural evil invoked by his tenants' curses germinated in Mr Sufi's mind. It was a fact that everywhere landlords were regarded with ill-will by tenants who suffered from the chronic delusion that they were being swindled, and it was also a fact that their wealth and social standing aroused envy and hate. How else could his misfortune be explained? Gool, Abu-salaam, Mr Rahim, Faizel Adil, the thieves who stole the lamps, were all tied in a conspiracy against him. Of course they were not conscious that they were acting collectively against him. Even Fawzia's aborted love-affair could be explained on the basis of a supernaturally-inspired conspiracy. She had led a secluded life, never harmed anyone nor committed any evil. She was an innocent victim because she was his daughter. As for Faizel Adil, his very nature was inhuman; he was surely not himself when he set out on his knave's course. Gool himself, the man who had set evil into motion against him, was not to blame; he was merely the agent of some sort of unearthly Dracula. Therefore his attempt to marshall the help of the supermen of the Spartan Gymnasium had been doomed from the beginning. Even Mr Rahim, an otherwise charming man, had found himself filled with irrational hate for one who provided him with shelter. All the evidence suggested that he was the object of a visitation, and his only resource against it was to enlist the aid of men who were capable of pacifying the forces of, evil. He would consult Molvi Haroon, the priest at the Newtown mosque. An amulet of various appropriate extracts from the

74

Koran should successfully ward off all evil invoked by unbenign imprecations and perhaps the Molvi could also arrange some special prayer for him to perform. Convinced that these measures would bring an end to his misfortune, he resolved to seek the priest's aid.

The next day was Friday and he rose from bed earlier than usual. While having his bath, he considered whether he should consult Molvi Haroon at the mosque or at his home. If he spoke to the Molvi unceremoniously in the mosque gossip and suspicion could arise, and if he went to his home like a suppliant he would be demeaning himself. His best course was to invite the Molvi to lunch after prayers, and over lunch broach the matter. He emerged from the steaming bath and towelled himself briskly. He felt a certain glow and vigour returning to his body.

After leaving word with his wife that he would be bringing Molvi Haroon home for lunch, he went down to the basement, climbed into his Jaguar and drove towards the mosque.

It was no more than a few minutes from his house, and when he reached it he realised that noon prayers would not take place for an hour. He sauntered into the mosque yard and stood for a while gazing at the goldfish and the red water-lilies. He sat down on a bench beside an oleander tree. The tranquil atmosphere filled him with serenity and he decided to enter the mosque and spend his time reading the Koran until the congregation arrived and prayers began.

When he entered the mosque he was surprised to see Molvi Haroon seated in a corner reading the Koran. The Molvi glanced at him and went on reading. He saw a Koran on the window-sill, took it and squatted on the carpet. As he had never bothered to read the Koran since his youth when he had attended a religious seminary, he now found the Arabic alphabet meaningless and he began to be afflicted by doubts about his coming to the mosque earlier than usual. However, when he had read repeatedly the first chapter, which he knew by heart as it was the prelude to every prayer, the Arabic alphabet unlocked its mystery.

When people began arriving they looked at him, head bowed over the Koran, in surprise. They had seen him at Friday prayers, but this was the first time they had seen him arrive before them and sit down to read the Koran.

He had stopped reading a little while ago, though he kept his eyes focused on a page. He was debating how to approach Molvi

Haroon. Should he wait for him outside the mosque after prayers and then, as soon as he appeared, go up to him and invite him? Or should he stand close behind him during prayers and immediately afterwards take him by the arm proprietorially and lead him to his Jaguar? Both methods had this disadvantage: that they would draw the attention of the congregation and lead to speculation regarding his motives. Yet he could not delay in inviting him; there was the danger that someone else might do so first. There were always several people who wished to be hosts of the Molvi on a Friday.

More people entered the mosque, the muezzin went up the minaret to intone the call for prayers and the congregation was summoned. Mr Sufi stood behind Molvi Haroon and during prayers all his thoughts were concentrated on whether Molvi Haroon would accept the invitation which he intended making as soon as prayers were over.

When Molvi Haroon recited the final prayer, he braced himself to extend his hand in greeting. The prayer over, he rose from the carpet, but found himself prevented from moving forward by a heavy hand on his shoulder, the hand of the man who had prayed beside him — Gool! Gool took his hand and shook it and asked him how he was. Confused, in a state of panic, he did not know what to say, but was saved further bewilderment by Molvi Haroon who came up to them and greeted them.

'You must come home for lunch, Molvi Haroon,' Gool said in Gujarati before Mr Sufi could gather himself and articulate his invitation. Nevertheless, unable to curb the words springing to his lips, he extended his invitation, but the Molvi declined saying that he was religiously bound to accept the first one. Gool asked Mr Sufi to join them but he said his family would be waiting for him. The trio left the mosque and when they parted Mr Sufi saw Molvi Haroon entering Gool's Spider with what seemed like a derisive look at him. He felt bitterly piqued at being slighted. Surely the holy man should have given precedence to an honourable man's invitation?

Though thwarted by Gool, he was determined to consult the Molvi that day, and after a solitary lunch — his wife and children never dined with him — and an hour of aimless driving in his car, he drove to the Molvi's residence in Lovers' Walk.

The Molvi was pleased to see him. He was dressed in a blue cotton smock and looked even more dwarfish than when dressed

76

in his long coat, trousers and turban. That this physically stunted man — now looking so obsequious — had spurned his invitation rankled within him.

In the sitting-room Mr Sufi immediately confided, in Gujarati, his reason for the visit. Some misfortune had come his way and he wanted help.

'Yes,' the Molvi said, 'I will make up an amulet for you and also compile a schedule of prayers which you can recite at home without taking the trouble of coming to the mosque.'

Mr Sufi thought his last few words to be barbed with an implied jeer at his religious indifference.

'Is there any fee, Molvi Haroon?'

'There is no fee, brother Sufi. But should you wish to offer a gift there is no restrictive law in Islamic jurisprudence.'

'I should like to reward you,' he said, as an idea unfolded in his mind. 'When can I come to collect the amulet and the schedule of prayers?'

'Let me see . . . Monday morning should do.'

Mr Sufi took leave, chuckling at the idea occupying his mind.

On Monday morning he told his wife to instruct one of the housemaids to take a box of lamps from the guests' room and place it in his car.

He drove to the Molvi's residence. The Molvi gave him the amulet and the schedule of prayers, and also, as a special favour, recited a prayer for his welfare and happiness. When he had ended, Mr Sufi said:

'I went to a sale last week and bought some lamps. I want to give you some as a gift.'

The Molvi thanked him gratefully, though he seemed somewhat surprised at the nature of the gift.

'Will you tell your housemaid to come with us to the car outside.'

They went outside. The maid took the box of lamps and placing it on her head — much to the consternation of Mr Sufi, who thought it a risky way of conveying fragile (and stolen!) things — serenely carried it into the house.

He shook hands with the Molvi and left. He felt satisfied at his courage in giving away a box of the lamps. In future he would not allow people to impose on him; he would impose on them. His problems, he decided, were largely due to his lack of those qualities of firm resolution and positive action so vital in achieving

77

success in this world, as the cinema screen so often testified.

When he reached home he tied the amulet, a black cloth satchet containing relevant extracts from the Koran, around his neck so that it hung like a pendant. Then he called the housemaids and boldly ordered them to remove the lamps from the guests' room and store them in a vacant corner in the basement.

It was at this time that he made a surprising discovery. On each box appeared the inscription: Atlas Electrical Company. Contents: 100 Apollo lamps. He recalled that the figure 200 had entered his calculation during the night the lamps arrived. If only he had known the correct figure then! What a price he had paid for his error in terms of redoubled inner stress and mental attrition! The discovery reinforced his determination to respond positively to life.

One night while parking his car in the basement after returning from the cinema, it occurred to him that he could easily take several boxes of lamps in one of his cars into the country and there throw them over a precipice into a hollow. He quickly placed six boxes in the boot of his largest car, a Chrysler, and drove out. He was gripped by elation. He would spend the night transporting the lamps out of the city.

He drove along the highway. When he reached open country he turned onto a gravel road and drove on. The road went down a slope and past some gigantic boulders. When he neared a bend in the road he saw in the yellow shafts of the headlights a cluster of ruined huts beside some trees. He drove cautiously over a track towards the huts. The headlights showed broken walls, thatched roofs that had partly fallen, pieces of rusted zinc among some debris. He stopped near the huts, got out of the car, and opening the boot took a box of lamps and carried it into a hut. After he had placed all the boxes in the hut he drove back home. On his second journey he brought ten boxes; he placed some on the rear seat of the car.

He made several more journeys until he had brought all the boxes. He placed some in each of the huts, covered them with pieces of zinc and then carefully concealed them with wads of roof straw. Satisfied that the lamps would be safe for some time he returned home. Had he thrown them down from some precipice he would have felt unhappy about their wasteful destruction. Now perhaps someone would find them, tell the owner of the farm, and he would return them to the manufacturers.

When he reached home it was .past three in the morning. He went into the guests' room and switched on the lights. He sat down in an armchair and was filled with a profound sense of relief. The incubus that had usurped his guests' room had at last been dispelled.

In his bedroom he took a vow that he would undertake the obligatory pilgrimage to Mecca as soon as his affairs were settled. Now that the lamps were out of the way, he was in a position to stop Gool continuing to blackmail him. If necessary he would have him indicted in court; the cheques he had drawn would be sufficient evidence to have him imprisoned for a long time. Before going to bed, he read the 'Prayer before sleeping' prescribed in the schedule. He slept peacefully and dreamt about Olga.

The next day was a happy one for Mr Sufi. He went to the cinema as usual and enjoyed himself. He felt that he was on the verge of regaining his former life with all its pleasures. In the evening he decided to go in search of Olga.

Since the incident in 'Nirvana Mansions' he had thought of her several times. He had not fully appreciated her when he could possess her at will. Now her absence magnified her loveliness of character rather than her mellow body: her considerate nature, her soft speech, her courtesy. She had been the gentlest of his concubines. Even when he had told her of his intention to separate from her 'for a while' she had not lost her pacific temper (as had some of the other women, who had turned upon him with fury). And before she had left her apartment she had written a letter to him thanking him for keeping her and telling him that she would be staying with a sister in Fountain Road. Olga was the only woman he had ever thought of marrying as his second wife, but the fear that she too might bear him daughters had deterred him. He now longed to see her and to spend a few hours in her company.

He went to Fountàin Road where a few homes seemed to be strangled by manufacturers' buildings and motor-car repair shops. He knocked at the door of a house and inquired. He was told that Olga lived across the road.

The house was a grey wooden structure on a concrete foundation. He entered a rusted gate and began to feel a little afraid. How would she receive him? He stood in front of the door, wondering whether he should not return home. Perhaps she was living with a man and he might find himself in an embarrassing situation. But his longing to meet her flowed strongly and reminding himself of his commitment to positive action he knocked at the door.

A young girl opened the door. He smiled in relief and said he wished to speak to Olga.

'Come in,' she said.

He looked into a dingy passage and hesitated.

'Come in,' she said again.

He entered. There was a curtained doorway on the left to which the girl pointed.

He parted the faded curtain and entered the room. He sat down on a chair, hearing a voice and the tramp of heavy feet on the wooden floor. A woman appeared through the curtain.

'Hullo,' she said. 'Olga will come in a minute. She is in the bathroom. What is your name?'

He told her and she left.

He waited, overjoyed that he had found her. He examined the room. There was a settee beside the chair he was sitting on; some of the cushion covers were torn and the plastic foam extruded. There was a display cabinet with a tarnished trophy of sorts and an antique photograph of an old woman. On the wall hung a faded bamboo scroll with a drawing of a Chinese rural scene.

He heard footsteps and Olga entered the doorway in a night-dress, with her hair turbaned in a towel to take the damp out.

'Olga!' he said, rising from the chair and taking her hand.

They sat down on the settee. Olga was glad to see him. He asked her about her health, what work she was doing, and whether she sometimes recalled old days. The poverty of the home in which she lived made him concerned about her welfare. She was no longer a physical body for his pleasure, but a complex being with a life of her own.

Before he left he asked her to meet him the next morning. He wished to take her out into the country for a drive.

She was waiting for him outside the house in Fountain Road. They drove out of the city southwards. When the highway came to an end they found themselves passing through valleys, skirting wooded ridges. He saw a gravel road branch away towards his left and turned the car to follow it. The road ascended a brow of rising ground, then plunged towards a forest, passing through its shade. He turned off the road and drove slowly among the trees, avoiding fallen branches and stones. He stopped his car in a clearing.

Throughout the journey he had spoken little and Olga had sat quietly beside him admiring the passing landscape.

'Shall we take a walk?' she asked.

He agreed and they walked among the trees. He held her hand. The answering pressure of her fingers expressed her warm regard for him.

They passed through the trees into a glade. The sun was hidden by the clouds. A delicious coolness filled the air. There was bird-song on all sides. They sat down on the fallen trunk of a tree and spoke to each other. Olga told him that she had worked as a factory hand for a short period after they had separated and now depended on her sister. He told her of 'certain financial and other problems' that had beset him, but were now, he was happy to say, in recession. She listened to him with sympathy and sensitive understanding and said that she looked to the day when he would be happy again. He realised Olga as a person now, a person whose worth transcended the pleasure she could give.

She had brought a picnic basket. She spread a cloth on the grass and they ate.

At noon they returned to the city.

In the afternoon Molvi Haroon telephoned to enquire how his affairs were getting on. Mr Sufi told him that they were improving and that he hoped the confidence he had placed in the Molvi would be kept secret. The Molvi assured him of his honour in such matters, and then informed him that a deputation from the Crescent Charitable Trust would be happy to have an audience with such a distinguished Muslim as he was. He readily agreed. Several years before a deputation from the same organisation had approached him for a donation, but he had refused to give one on the ground that he was assisting many other organisations in Durban and Cape Town. He had of course not mentioned that he did not consider charity to be a virtue as it generally confirmed in the lazy their bad habit of relying on others. Now he wished to offer them a donation. There was the possibility that his meanness had been a contributory factor in the genesis of the visitation which had afflicted his life. He was now presented with the opportunity of purging himself of a blemish and so clearing the way for the better working of beneficent influences. In fact the arrival of the opportunity to exercise generosity was in itself a manifestation of the working of such influences.

The deputation arrived in the evening. Accompanying Molvi Haroon were Mr Darsot, the spice merchant, Mr Khaled, an accountant, and Hajji Suleiman the draper whose flowing henna-red beard was perfumed with attar. Mr Sufi, after shaking their hands cordially, invited them to enter the guests' room which was now open to visitors again. The deputation observed the warmth with which Mr Sufi received them in contrast with his coldness on the first occasion.

Molvi Haroon began with a recital from the Koran of various extracts and then went on to explain in Gujarati the Prophet's concept of wealth as a stewardship on which the poor had a rightful claim. He concluded by reciting other extracts that promised paradise to those who cared for orphans and widows.

When he ended Mr Sufi said:

'I am having some financial problems, but I will give a donation.'

'In this world none of us are exempt from difficulties,' Mr Darsot said. 'We could come at a later date.'

Molvi Haroon, sensing the danger in Mr Darsot's words, said quickly in Arabic and then translated into Gujarati:

'Allah blesses those most who give when they themselves are in need.'

'Is there any specific sum you need?' Mr Sufi asked, taking out his cheque book from his coat pocket.

Hajji Suleiman looked at Mr Darsot (who was the chairman of the Trust) as if to say he should not let the opportunity slip and stipulate a sum. Mr Darsot, however, knowing Mr Sufi to be a man who kept a close grip on his wealth, feared to frighten him by mentioning a sum. The man had agreed to give them a donation; that was sufficient. They could always approach him later again.

'No specific sum, brother Sufi. We will be satisfied with whatever you give.'

'Remember,' Molvi Haroon said, 'that our Prophet was an orphan and spoke on many occasions of the special blessings that would come to those who gave charity without caring about their personal welfare.'

Mr Sufi wrote out a cheque for a very large sum of money, feeling that the multiplex force of the digits would help to fend off the visitation. He handed the cheque to Mr Darsot. Mr Darsot felt a sudden contraction within him for he himself had never given the Trust such a large sum of money. He handed the cheque to Molvi Haroon who smiled, showing his paan-reddened teeth. He passed on the cheque to Hajji Suleiman who, after hastily taking out his spectacles from his coat pocket, examined it with trembling hands. Mr Khaled, on receiving the cheque, looked at it with professional indifference.

Molvi Haroon then cupped his hands in thanksgiving prayer and exultingly read several extracts from the Koran. Everyone cupped their hands and looked reverent.

When Molvi Haroon ended Mr Sufi tinkled a bell and Fawzia and the kitchen maid arrived with tea and sweetmeats.

Before the deputation left Molvi Haroon offered a short prayer for Mr Sufi's prosperity and happiness.

For Mr Sufi the next two days came to approximate those scherzo times (the darkness of his recent life gave the past the dimension of a golden legend) when his life sparkled with women, motor-cars, cinemas, food, friends, and a matured bank account. Feeling confident that the combined force of the amulet, prayers, and his positive approach to life would soon bring back lost times, he visited friends and chose not to take seriously the alienation that had crept in since the ripening of his relationship with Gool. He spoke to his wife on several matters unconnected with their domestic life and gaily proposed a country excursion with the children on a bright Sunday. And to ensure that he was purged of all moral blemish he re-read all the letters (fortunately secreted in a drawer in his office) appealing to his charity: letters from individuals, schools, religious seminaries, orphanages, the Red Cross, sports clubs, political organisations (which he had always loathed and regarded as the creation of disaffected psychopathic individuals). He wrote out the cheques in a mood of almost hysterical benevolence. When he had signed the last cheque he thought of Olga. He wrote out a cheque for her and attached a note to it thanking her for her concern for him and for the happy day he had spent in her company. He went to the Central Road post office in the evening when the pavement was deserted and before posting the cheques read the prescriptive prayer from the schedule entitled 'Before doing anything important'. When the last cheque went into the scarlet mouth of the pillar-box, he felt that he had finally suffocated the dragon which had plagued his life.

The next day being Friday, Mr Sufi went to mosque as usual. Molvi Haroon saw him after prayers, went up to him and said:

'How are your affairs getting on, Sufi Sahib?'

'Very well, Molvi Haroon. You have been very helpful. Already there is a change.'

'Allah be praised.'

He was about to take his leave, fearing that if Gool saw them he would come up to them, when Molvi Haroon detained him by placing his hand on his shoulder and saying:

'The lamps you gave me were very useful, Sufi Sahib. Some of the lamps in the chandeliers of the mosque were burnt out, so I replaced them with those you gave me.'

Mr Sufi looked up at the glittering crystal chandeliers hanging above him, and gazed at them as though he saw, at a great height in the heavens, the glowing fires of hell. If Molvi Haroon had looked at him then, he would have seen a bloodless face seized by terror and pain.

'I must go,' he muttered feebly and hastily left the mosque. His sudden descent into spiritual damnation came like the blast of the anger of God. He was damned, eternally damned for having given a holy man stolen lamps which were now illuminating a sacred place. He had sinned against God himself by desecrating His sanctum. Of what use was the amulet and schedule of prayers now? He could never return to the mosque, for its very chandeliers would expose him — to God, to himself and everyone else — as a diabolical creature consigned to eternal perdition.

He went home, trembling in anguished confusion, his hope crushed.

Fifteen

Over the telephone Gool's words pierced like slivers into Mr Sufi's ears:

'There is trouble for you. Come over to High Road immediately.'

'Trouble?'

'Yes. Serious. There is danger over the telephone.'

He held the telephone in his hand for a while, disbelieving the doom-crack message. He went to his bedroom and sat down on the edge of the bed. Gool's words signalled the onset of final earthly calamity, a calamity he had secretly, fearfully known to be approaching — he had felt within him its destructive pulse — since the lamps began to burn in the Newtown mosque. He thought of suicide, of catapulting himself in his Jaguar over a cliff. But the thought was sterile. Gool's hold over him denied him even the freedom to destroy himself.

Later he roused himself, went down the stairs to his car, and drove to High Road.

Gool met him with his usual smile.

'Come into the office, Mr Sufi.'

Gool sat down at his desk. Mr Sufi sat on a chair facing him.

'You are in serious trouble.'

Mr Sufi looked down at his feet, his voice strangled. A coldness, bursting out from some Arctic frontier within, flooded his trembling body.

'There is trouble over the lamps. By the way they must be very useful to you. You will have lights in your mansions for the rest of your life.'

He felt like saying that the lamps had darkened his life, but could not articulate the words. The thought suffused him with gloom, a gloom that seemed to swell into a monstrous mushroom before his eyes.

'Your stairs are beautifully lit. No one need ever stumble in the dark again.'

'Yes,' he said timidly, almost in a whisper, as though affirming to himself the folly of having kept his stairs unlit. His gloom overwhelmed and smothered the tumult that usually swirled within him whenever any reference was made to unlit stairs. Gool appeared to him now like some hero of the cinema, taking revenge on behalf of tenants faced with the ordeal of ascending and descending stairs at night.

'The lamps have a lovely name. Do you remember it?'

Mr Sufi tried to recall the name, but failed. The statue of Apollo, however, came to life in his mind's eye. The god frowned and gently flung a lamp at him for failing to recall his name. The lamp burst like a bubble as it reached him.

The vision dissolved and he heard Gool say, musingly:

'Apollo . . . a beautiful Greek god . . . beautiful.'

In a state of abject depression, Mr Sufi found Gool's obsession with Apollo meaningless. The days of the pagan deities had long passed and he failed to see what they had to do with the reality of modern electrical lamps.

'To get to the trouble, the police have arrested them.'

'Arrested?'

'Yes. They have confessed . . . those who delivered the lamps. There is a warrant of arrest against you.'

Mr Sufi flung his head back and his arms upwards as though warding off the blows of an attacker and shrieked as though several skewers were being plunged into various parts of his body.

Gool jumped up from his chair, filled a glass with liquor and poured it into his mouth.

Mr Sufi choked and coughed and gasped. He shouted, 'No! No! No!' and rushed round the room, feeling weirdly legless, a torso whirled in a surrealist tempest. Broken, blinded, imprisoned in some torture chamber without hope of release, he pleaded miserably: 'No . . . Don't let them . . . Gool . . . I beg . . . Don't let them.' The room spun in feverish merry-go-round; desk and cupboard and cabinet and chairs seemed to be animated missiles charging at him, and Gool a many-faced spider pursuing him, constricting him, striking him.

When, after what seemed a timeless interval, he emerged from the hurly-burly of his convulsive experience, he found himself seated in a chair, exhausted and sweating, with Gool offering him more liquor. He sipped the liquor and felt calm returning. Gool assuaged him by saying:

'There is nothing to worry about. They will never arrest you while I am alive. Captain Green was here this morning and tore up the warrant before my eyes.'

His fears dissolved and euphoria bloomed within him. While he was under Gool's 'protection' he was safe. He looked at Gool with admiration. Nothing would ever crack his imperturbable spirit.

'You know how to manage things.'

'Yes, but I think the Captain expects a reward.'

He produced his cheque book.

'We must remember he carries out orders,' Gool said. 'There are others, his superiors. Even the magistrate.'

'How much do you think?'

'We cannot offer too much in the beginning. But eventually we must compromise. Give me a blank cheque and I will give them the minimum possible.'

He signed a cheque, handed it to Gool and left the room.

In the street Mr Sufi entered his Jaguar. All the sap seemed to have run out of his body, leaving him like a bleached corpse rolling down a sand dune. He went home, crept into bed and slept through the day and night.

Towards dawn he dreamt of Apollo. The god stood beside him and said in Gool's voice:

'You are in serious trouble . . . You will have lights in your mansion for the rest of your life . . . Your stairs are beautifully lit . . . No one need ever stumble in the dark again.'

He awoke in fear and drew the curtains beside his bed so that the pale morning light entered. The words lingered in his mind. Had Gool told him the truth? Could he be in 'serious trouble' and also have lights in his mansions for the rest of his life? Had there been a warrant of arrest? Had Gool tricked him into giving him a blank cheque?

During the next few days Mr Sufi reviewed his desperate situation.

Since the time when his involvement with Gool had gone beyond the threshold of the early 'protection' period, he had been driven into the labyrinth of schizophrenic distraction. Socially, his status and respectability were irrevocably lost. Many people avoided him, and when meetings were unavoidable they showed no eagerness to speak to him. His friends had stiffened. He was an untouchable. There had been a time, he recalled, when days were serene and nights imbued with the charm of love. He was now a recluse within his agony, a prisoner in the void of inner exile, unable even to find comfort in those nearest him, his wife and children. To Fawzia, caught in the vortex of his affairs, he had brought mildew, damaging her young life. Morally he was contaminated: he had drunk liquor, which was forbidden; he had joined in a debauch and led two of his former concubines to sinful fornication, and he had been a party to the violence committed in 'Nirvana Mansions'. Spiritually he was damned by the sacrilegious burning of the lamps in the chandeliers of the Newtown mosque from which he had excommunicated himself for ever. Criminally he was implicated in a theft, perpetually exposed to the threat of arrest. And, finally, threatening doom, his financial empire was reeling: the digits in his bank account that buttressed it were tumbling, and the revenue from his apartment buildings was diminishing for many of his tenants, either unable or unwilling to pay the inflated rents imposed by him, or fearing his association with a dangerous man, were beginning to leave.

Sixteen

Several months later, while Mr Sufi was having breakfast, the telephone rang. Gool informed him that he had an 'exciting proposal' to make to him that would convert him into a millionaire in a short time. He should come to High Road where he would give him the details.

He left his breakfast unfinished, went to his bedroom and sat down on the edge of the bed. The 'proposal' aroused no excitement in him. For a week now he had made his bedroom his hermitage; it was here, on the pretext that he suffered from migraine, that he spent long hours, garrotted by defeat, loneliness and self-pity.

Yet, as he lay in bed, all his wants solicitously anticipated by his wife and daughter, listening to their voices as they went about their domestic duties, he came to realise that only in relation to them did his life take on meaning. His wife's love for him had been expressed not by word, but by her silent devotion to his well-being. On a profounder level, he gradually became conscious of the beauty of his wife and children — not only of their physical beauty but also of the primary beauty of their beings to which he was emotionally, spiritually and organically united. A yearning to have them near him seized him: he wanted them to sit beside him and talk to him, even about the most trivial of matters. Several times he attempted to draw them into conversation, but their respect for him made them listeners rather than participants. He rued his decision to banish his wife from his bed, for now he was overcome by that natural yet most profound of human longings: to hold another being's hands. And what intensified his agony was that, while all he need say to his wife was that she should return and she would do so unhesitatingly, he could not do so: his will had snapped. Especially the voices of his daughters, ringing with innocence and happiness as they played on the balcony, affected him deeply: he craved to hold them in his arms and kiss them. At such moments came the crushing realisation of their mortality: they would grow up, eventually grow old and one day perish. This thought wrung his being with such inordinate sharp bitter anguish that he was filled with overwhelming compassionate love for them.

Later he went to see Gool.

'You have heard of Elysia,' Gool said to him as soon as they were seated, each with a glass of brandy in his hand. 'I have spoken to a lawyer about you and his opinion is that the best way of multiplying your wealth is to invest in land in Elysia.'

Mr Sufi sipped the liquor and felt a raw sensation in his gullet.

'If you think I am trying to make you invest in something worthless, then let us go and consult a lawyer. You can decide afterwards.'

He had read in the newspapers of Elysia and the government's plans to make it an exclusive area for Asians. Under the plan all properties in Fordsburg would be expropriated and sold to whites. Controversy had raged in the press regarding the motive behind the Group Areas Act, and the Orient Front and the People's Movement had condemned Elysia as a racial ghetto. He had attended a meeting of property owners to decide on a course of action. It had been a rowdy meeting, for some tenants also turned up with placards proclaiming in scarlet: 'It is your turn to be evicted now!'; 'The end of tyranny by landlords!' ; 'Our own homes in Elysia!'. Some of his former tenants shouted his name jeeringly and made obscene gestures at him. The eccentric landlord Joosub appeared at the meeting in Arab garb. He was accompanied by two of his servants dressed as Cape coons, whom he declared to be his 'lawyers'. He insisted on praying on the stage in the hall and there was silence while he performed the usual genuflections. When he had finished he announced that he had received a divine message that if all landlords stopped accepting rent from tenants, Allah would send his archangel Gibrail to settle matters. He was wildly applauded by the tenants. Then he lapsed into silence and sat on the stage flanked by his two 'lawyers'. The meeting ended with a resolution to petition the rulers to grant an extension of five years before they began to expropriate properties. Though Mr Sufi had consented to the resolution he had remained silent. Even without the government's threat he would have been compelled to sell some of his properties to keep himself financially buoyant, and the sale would have given rise to questioning, gossip and humiliation. Now he was presented with a reason for selling them, and even though he risked accusations of betrayal by fellow landlords, he would be able to stand up to them. Ultimately the government's bulldozers would triumph.

Shortly after Mr Sufi had returned home from the meeting, four young men came to see him. As soon as they were seated in the guests' room Ebrahim, the leader of the group, said:

'We are members of the People's Movement.'

He looked at them critically. They were a racial motley; they were dressed gaudily; their hair was long, giving them the appearance of nubile girls; they carried themselves like arrogant braggarts.

'Is there anything I can do for you?'

'Nothing for us, but for yourself.'

He was mystified. Had these hermaphrodites been sent by some secret People's Court to fetch him? Or were they merely a gang of freaks and perverts out to rag him?

'We are here to help you,' Ebrahim said. 'You know about Elysia. We intend to launch protest rallies.'

His imagination lit up a multitude of people, anarchists, nihilists, communists, snaking through streets, holding aloft banners, and shouting slogans.

'To help me?'

'Yes, of course. Your properties are in danger. We intend to stand by you.'

'I am afraid I don't take part in politics.'

His answer elicited a rapid fire of questions from the quartet.

'You are not interested in what happens to you?'

'You want to be evicted?'

'You wish to be destroyed?'

'You refuse to accept our aid?'

He cringed.

'Gentlemen, I inherited . . .'

'Inherited or not, they are yours,' Ebrahim interrupted. 'We intend protecting you from the Herrenvolk landlords.'

'The bloodsuckers!'

'The Caesars!'

'The fascists!'

A moment of silence followed. Then Ebrahim went on, in a conciliatory tone:

'Mr Sufi, please understand that we represent the oppressed people and have to carry out our responsibilities. We are your friends, though you may not think so. We are prepared to sacrifice our lives for you.'

'I understand,' he whispered, touched.

'Now you are reacting as a true son of Liberty. You will appreciate that resistance goes hand in glove with the instruments of resistance. What I mean is that we need funds to help us in the struggle to help you. You know how we operate. We need money for paper, duplicating machines, premises; we have to hold conferences, transport delegates and supporters; then there are lawyers' fees, bail and other expenses that run into thousands.'

He felt awed at the vast protest machinery that was to be set in motion for his sake. He wrote out a cheque quickly and handed it to Ebrahim.

'You will understand that the sacrifices we are making cannot be counted in terms of money,' Ebrahim said, taking the cheque, glancing at its value and tearing it into confetti. 'We spend our lives trying to protect innocent people like you. It is certain you will be eaten up by the Herrenvolk shark if you don't help us to help you.'

Mr Sufi saw himself in a sea of blood. He took his pen and wrote out another cheque.

Gool was about to lead the way out of his office when he said, turning:

'Come see what I bought yesterday.'

Gool went towards a shelf, opened a cardboard box and carefully removed a statuette of Apollo.

'I was passing an art shop yesterday when I saw it in the window.'

He placed the statuette on a small semi-circular table.

'I would give anything in the world to look like him,' Gool said in admiration.

Mr Sufi looked at Gool. The man was obviously obsessed by an image. But it occurred to him that perhaps Gool's good fortune in life was a result of his adoration of an idol. With a feeling of personal inadequacy he examined the statuette.

'That's Apollo,' he whispered.

The beauty of the god, of the ideal human form thrust itself upon his awareness.

'Whenever I look at Apollo I think of lamps,' Gool said.

Mr Sufi was brought trenchantly back to himself, and to the tumour within.

The lawyer's office was in Fox Street. When they entered the reception room they were met by a slender lady with blond curls and blue eyes. She greeted them and led the two men through a carpeted passage to a glass door.

The lawyer was seated behind a large table. He had a round face, fleshy cheeks, curly hair and a small beard. He reminded Mr Sufi of a goblin who had run away from the woods and usurped a modern office of filing cabinets, an oak table laden with the usual pens, papers and files, and shelves filled with formidable phalanxes of books.

'Sit down, gentlemen. I am at your service.'

'Mr Mohamed, this is Mr Sufi,' Gool said.

'I am very happy to meet you, Mr Sufi. As you know I am an adviser to many property owners. By my advice many a man has become wealthy. Though unluckily for me my fate is that of all advisers. We are soon forgotten. Sometimes we are killed.'

He laughed in a series of sharp muted barks.

'When I was at school,' Mr Mohamed continued, 'I acted the part of Polonius and was killed by Hamlet.'

'You will be killed again,' Gool said facetiously, 'if you don't tell Mr Sufi of the advantages of buying land in Elysia.'

He laughed again.

'My advice to you, Mr Sufi, is to buy land now. The petition by property owners is not going to succeed. Mr Mia and Mr Darsot have realised this and submitted their applications. Several properties in Fordsburg are already up for sale to whites. Look at these.'

There was a file on his table. He opened it and showed Mr Sufi some newspaper advertisements.

'I speak as an authority on the Group Areas Act. Within two

93

years land prices in Elysia will rocket and you could be a millionaire. Land is power, that is a legal saying. Have you visited Elysia?'

'Let us go there now,' Gool said.

'Excellent! My other clients can wait.'

He lifted the telephone.

'Tell John to bring the car.'

The lawyer rose from his chair and his clients followed him. In the reception room he introduced them to Helena, the lady who had met them on arrival. She was dressed in a grey silk blouse and a short blue skirt. Around her neck were two strings of multi-coloured beads.

'Helena is a descendant of Helen of Troy,' Mr Mohamed said jocosely.

She answered with a smile, her scarlet lips revealing rows of even teeth.

Mr Sufi recalled the classical Helen. A year ago he had seen the film — Gool had seen it too, at the Lyric — entitled 'The Face that Launched a Thousand Ships'.

'Mr Sufi is an important figure in the community, Helena,' the lawyer said. 'You are going to see a great deal of him.'

'That will be lovely.' And she smiled at Mr Sufi, who stood near her.

'By the way, how many sisters have you?' the lawyer asked.

'Two.'

'Three Helens!' Gool exclaimed. 'When can we meet the other two?'

'Any time.'

'Mr Sufi, our luck is in,' Gool said smilingly.

'To Elysia now, on business,' the lawyer said, moving towards the door. 'Later, maybe this weekend, we shall abduct the three virgins.'

Helena made an arch enquiry and there was merriment. Mr Sufi managed a smile.

'Helena, lock the door and come with us,' the lawyer said as they stepped out onto the pavement.

In the street a car was waiting for them, the doors open.

Mr Mohamed sat next to the chauffeur. Helena sat between Gool and Mr Sufi. On the way to Elysia Mr Mohamed spoke of the bright future that awaited Mr Sufi.

'Our politicians can go on protesting, but you are among the fortunate few . . . '

As the car passed through the city and reached open country Mr Sufi began to feel like a condemned prisoner taking his last ride. The bronze rocks along the roadside, the sentinel-like trees in rain-blessed sunlit fields, and perfumed Helena beside him (with her hands, languid and heavy with rings, in her lap, her left thigh nestling against his) reminded him of tranquil evenings in the apartments of his concubines, of mornings when the bathroom tap gurgled and the aroma of breakfast filled the kitchen, of days that held undiluted promise.

They reached Elysia after an hour and got out of the car. In the distance was a low mountain range; below its slopes were clusters of homes that formed part of the government's resettlement housing scheme. On their right was a wood of acacias.

'Beautiful virgin land,' Mr Mohamed said.

'What is the price of land here?' Mr Sufi asked.

'It is not expensive when compared to other areas. Can you see our city on the horizon? It is marching south.'

'I haven't sufficient capital,' Mr Sufi said regretfully.

'That's no problem. I can sell your properties immediately to whites and raise the money. Let me handle your affairs for you, Mr Sufi. I shall do my best since you are a friend of Mr Gool.'

A paradise widow bird flew past, trailing its long black tail. They looked at it.

'Leave everything in Mr Mohamed's hands,' Gool advised Mr Sufi. 'You cannot leave it in my hands. I might be killed at any moment by my enemies.'

Gool's words, though spoken in a matter-of-fact tone, reverberated painfully within Mr Sufi.

Mr Mohamed now went on to speak of the link between wealth and land and concluded with these words: 'History offers us this lesson: when men are without land they are lost.'

'Then they have to look for a bonfire to throw themselves in,' Gool said laughing.

'Or find comfort in a woman's arms,' Helena said, smiling at Mr Sufi.

Mr Sufi walked several paces away from the group. He looked at the fields before him and at the serene expanse of the sky and experienced for a moment (though he was urban in his soul) a feeling of communion with natural beauty.

Several yellow birds flashed past on whirring wings and Mr Sufi

95

rejoined the group.

'Mr Mohamed, I think you can put my properties up for sale.'

'I congratulate you on your decision,' the lawyer said, placing his arm over Mr Sufi's shoulder. 'Let us now return to the city and business.'

And Mr Sufi got into the car.

The noise of the city overtook them suddenly. They were in the midst of shining motor-cars, roaring excavators, screeching drills, blaring hooters, coloured neon signs, scurrying pedestrians. The car swung around a corner and came to a stop.

In the lawyer's office all the relevant documents were prepared after Mr Sufi had gone home and brought a briefcase full of papers. The details were checked with municipal records by telephone. They adjourned to a nearby restaurant for lunch and returned to complete their business. Mr Sufi signed the documents with Helena and Gool as witnesses. By the time they had finished an hour remained before dusk.

'Gool,' Mr Mohamed said, 'I think we need some diversion after the day's work.'

'Let's go to High Road and have supper,' said Gool.

'Helena,' Mr Mohamed said, 'you go with John and bring your two sisters to Gool's place. We'll meet you there.'

The three men went to High Road. They sat in the lounge and drank wine, waiting for the arrival of Helena and her companions. The lawyer spoke of the bright future that awaited Mr Sufi, and went on to say:

'Of course the sale of your properties will realise more money than will bé needed to buy land. The surplus can be used in a number of ways. For instance, we could invest in shares yielding high-percentage returns. We could also . . . '

By the time Helena and her companions arrived Mr Sufi was feeling convivial. Cheryl was a tall, rather gawky brunette with a bronzed skin and Josephine a small, buxom woman, much made-up.

Supper was served on a candle-lit table. After supper they returned to the lounge for coffee, liqueurs and cigars or cigarettes. Mr Sufi showed keen interest in the ladies and when Mr Mohamed proposed that they should all go picnicking on a Sunday, Mr Sufi reminded him:

'You know what you said today before we went to Elysia? "We shall abduct the three virgins." '

Everyone laughed.

Later that night the three women were taken home. They lived in an apartment on the tenth floor of a building in Hillbrow. The men were invited up for a drink. The building was modern and the apartment carpeted, centrally heated and well-furnished. While having drinks Mr Sufi thought of his own buildings and felt happy that he had decided to sell them. They were disgracefully ugly and not worth possessing. He had spent his entire life guarding them as though they were strongholds of treasure. He felt grateful to Gool and the lawyer for convincing him that it was time to sell them. In Elysia he would own an apartment building like the one he was in; in fact he would have several such buildings erected.

'Friends,' he said, 'one day we shall all live in a beautiful building in Elysia.'

'Excellent!' Gool exclaimed, and applauded. They all applauded.

'I promise,' Mr Sufi continued, moved, 'that I shall share my wealth with you. You are all my friends.' ·

They applauded again and Gool rose to go.

'Ladies, good-night. We shall meet again.'

'No, you cannot go yet, ' Helena said to Mr Sufi, hanging on to him.

The others encircled them as she pressed her lips to his.

Mr Mohamed was taken home first, then Gool. Finally, Mr Sufi returned to 'Orient Mansions'.

It had been a long, eventful day for him, beginning with the visit to the lawyer and ending in the company of the three women. A variety of emotional states and inner movements, ranging from the penumbral misery in his bedroom to the sudden gust of sensual energy from Helena's lips, had pulsed through him. In one day he seemed to have passed through an age of living.

He stood for a while in the foyer of the building where he had spent so many years. It would soon be sold and later crushed to rubble by the sledgehammers of demolishers. It had been the nave of his life-pattern. He felt that in some way he had betrayed the building, that its eventual destruction was the result, not of a government order, but of a personal inability to protect it. The sense of betrayal worked on him as he walked up the illuminated stairs. He knew now the urban doom that awaited him, and the end of his days as an affluent landlord.

In his bedroom a surge of pessimism overwhelmed him. When it receded he felt that only as a derelict, freed of responsibility, of being, would he be able to evade determination by worldly things, preoccupation with his own fate, regret at times past, yearning for the nebula of the future, the power of Gool, the cunning of Mr Mohamed. Like flotsam driven by currents out at sea, he would go wherever life took him.

During the night sleep came to him fitfully, and dreams in morbidly garish colours reeled in his febrile brain . . . He was in a crowded arcade surrounded by howling, gyrating maenads . . . He was in Elysian fields where gay, one-legged nymphs romped beside pools echoing with weird laughter . . . He was in a wilderness where Apollo, standing on a granite crag, held aloft a flaming brand; where harpies shrieked obscenities in Helena's voice; where Mr Mohamed, his head impaled on the bonnet of his car, rushed vengefully towards him; where a smiling spider that was Gool looked on. Then the earth opened and he fell, down a screaming stair.

His wife found him lying helplessly on the floor, his face contorted. She flung herself down beside him and held him.

'What's the matter?' she cried. 'What's the matter?'

He clung to her, breathing convulsively, sweating profusely, seeking solace, compassion and love.

His cry awakened the children and they came into the room, frightened.

'Your father is ill,' their mother said. She caressed her husband's forehead tenderly for a while and then held his hands. He sat up, called his daughters to sit near him and touched them fondly.

'My children,' he said, looking at their beautiful faces.